Always

and

Forever

Always and Forever

By

Charles Embrey Jr

This book is a work of fiction. Names, characters, and incidents are a work and products of the author's imagination. Any resemblance to actual events, or persons, alive or dead, is purely coincidental. No animals, mythical, imaginary, or otherwise, were harmed or mistreated in any way during the writing of this book.

Always and Forever

Copyright ©2024 – Charles Embrey Jr. All rights reserved.

ISBN: 979-8-9864210-7-0

All rights reserved. This book may not be reproduced, in whole or in part, without the consent of the author.

GreyRealm Publishing

Hawesville, KY

Always and Forever

She had the face of an angel. It was the only way Ben could describe the newly arrived high school senior, as he sat enraptured in his fourth-period Anatomy class. The way she tossed her long golden hair when she laughed, the way her blue eyes sparkled, and her warm smile; it was all he could concentrate on.

He was abruptly shaken from his daydream by the class's laughter and Mr. Scott's voice. "Ben? Are you still with us Ben?"

Ben's cheeks flushed with embarrassment as he pushed his black, plastic-framed glasses back into place and looked up at Mr. Scott. "Sorry…I was up late studying." It was a feeble excuse but the best he could do in the moment.

"Oh, I see," replied the science teacher as he looked from Ben to the angel, and back again. He smiled at the boy and decided not to push further. Ben was, after all, one of his brightest and hardest-working students and had earned a reprieve.

Mr. Scott had been Ben's favorite teacher since Freshman Biology a few years ago. He also attended his class in Advanced Biology last year and now Anatomy and Physiology this, his senior year.

The young, energetic teacher was helping him prepare to take his MCAT for medical school and was sponsoring him for a national scholar award.

Mr. Scott's voice softened a bit, "I guess the midterm exams next week could cause a few sleepless nights. I was hoping you could sum up the exchange of gases in the lungs and the importance of oxygen concentration of inhaled room air."

Ben brightened as the class quieted down, but as the boy started to explain the marvel of human respiration, the bell signaled the end of class, and students scattered like roaches at midnight surprised by the kitchen light.

The clamor of the lunchroom drowned out Ben's thoughts as his two best friends, Sam, and Pete, plopped down across the table from him.

Pete, a lanky, awkward boy with sandy blonde hair, dropped his cafeteria tray on the brown, Formica tabletop, spilling his peas into his corn.

"Crap!" he loudly exclaimed as he looked disapprovingly at the mess he had made.

Sam laughed as she tossed her brown paper lunch sack on the table and sat.

Ben smiled but remained silent as he observed his friend's minor, self-imposed, misfortune.

"He is such a klutz," sighed Sam as she smiled back at Ben.

Sam, or Samantha, as her mom would call her, was shorter than her two male friends. Her dark brown hair and mischievous brown eyes were accentuated by her dark-framed glasses.

Ben and Sam had been fast friends since kindergarten. They had logged hundreds of miles all around the small town over the years and shared the joys of childhood and many birthday parties. Their parents and neighbors had always felt that they would end up as girlfriend and boyfriend but the two always felt more like brother and sister.

Pete and his family had moved to town about three years ago. On his first day of school, the skinny, awkward new kid found himself easy prey for the school's few bullies, but Ben and Sam swooped in for the rescue and they had become fast friends.

Always and Forever

"So, what was up with you in Anatomy class?" asked Pete, in between bites. "You were kinda spaced out."

"Oh," stammered Ben. "Just tired."

"Bull crap," exclaimed Sam with a half half-smile. "He was looking at the new girl. You can lie all you want Ben, but I saw you. Shoot, most of the class did."

Pete grinned broadly. "No kidding? I didn't see that. Well, keep dreaming buddy, cause that is as close as guys like you or I will ever get to a girl like that. I'd say out of our league, but she is more like out of our universe!"

"She's not that pretty," chimed in Sam with a slight hint of jealousy. "Besides Ben has a lot to offer."

"Yeah?" said Pete with a chuckle. "Maybe when he gets out of med school and becomes a rich neurosurgeon. Guys like us need a fat bank account to attract girls like them. Just look at Bill Gates."

Ben nervously laughed. "Pete's right Sam. Nerds need money."

The next week or so went by with Ben struggling to sit through Anatomy with the angel hopelessly on his mind.

Almost every day, the angel would be hit on in the hallway by some of the school's most popular guys, but all walked away frowning with their masculinity in question. She was an untouchable prize to the boys and each girl worried that it could be her boyfriend that would try next.

Ben was busy at his locker switching his books for his next class when a strong hand pulled him back by the shoulder. He turned to see the large, red, number twelve on a white football jersey. He looked up into the face of Greg Larson, obnoxious jerk, and starting varsity quarterback.

"Got an eye for the new girl, Lily, haven't ya?" asked the jock.

"I don't know what you're talking about," responded Ben awkwardly pushing his glasses up into place again.

"Sure, you do. Rumor has it you were practically drooling all over yourself back in Mr. Scott's class as you stared at her. Hey, I can't blame you. My source says he was surprised you could stand up when the bell rang. She is quite a looker."

"She is really pretty," said Ben sheepishly, not sure why Greg was taking time out of his busy social calendar to talk to him. "It's no use though; she'd never go for a guy like me."

"Well, you are quite the geek there, Four-eyes. But what if I could fix it?"

"What do you mean, 'fix it'?"

"I could have her eating out of your hand. She'd be all yours and would never even think of another guy. Yours and yours alone, forever."

"Thanks, Greg, but I have to get to my next class," replied Ben sarcastically as he turned to get his books.

The big quarterback pushed past Ben and slammed the locker shut. "Look Poindexter, I'm not yanking your chain here. Do me a simple favor and I promise to show you a way to make it happen. I guarantee it'll happen just as I said, or you can have the pink slip to my Firebird. I'll even let you hold on to it as proof."

Ben's eyes widened. "What favor?" he said, his voice dripping with skepticism.

"You and your geeky friends work in the office and help most of the teachers, right?"

Always and Forever

Ben nodded.

"Get me copies of the midterm exams by Friday and I'll fix it so Lily is out with you, melting in your arms, Saturday night and every other night after that."

Ben bit his lip and looked down at his feet. He had never done anything that could be considered unethical, dishonest, or illegal his entire life. Just the thought of it made his stomach hurt. "No. The answer is no!" he said firmly. "I can help you study but I won't help you cheat."

With renewed energy, Ben pushed past the quarterback and his buddies and resolutely headed for his next class.

Late that afternoon, the young scholar was unusually quiet as he and his friends pedaled towards their neighborhood. One of the pure pleasures of living in a smaller town was the lack of any hazardous traffic and older, quaint, well-kept homes lined the sleepy streets.

Ben's mind kept going over Greg's ridiculous offer. How in the world could he think Ben was so desperate that he would abandon all reason and be stupid enough to think the quarterback's offer was even possible? One thing was sure - the pink slip.

As Ben looked at his pedaling feet and over to his two friends as they rode along talking, the thought of driving the Firebird was appealing.

Voices in his head began to argue. "It would sure be nice to drive your friends right now and, what would it hurt to help Greg get through his exams?"

"Only your chance at med school, you idiot. If you get caught it could close the door to any scholarship and even acceptance itself."

"I'll see you two tomorrow!" shouted Pete as he peeled off down his street.

"Bye!" shouted Sam before she turned to Ben. "Okay, you, what's going on inside of that melon?"

"What?" said Ben defensively.

"Don't act like that with me. You have hardly said a word since we left school."

Ben sighed. Sam knew him better than anyone and he realized he needed to talk this out. "Greg Larson talked to me today."

"From the football team?"

He nodded and recounted the encounter at the lockers.

"How dumb can someone be? Does he honestly believe he can do that? If he has that kind of power, why doesn't he date her himself?"

"Yeah," nodded Ben in agreement. "But what about the car? I mean if he is dumb enough to offer it…?"

"True, but in all the years I have known you, you have never done anything like that. I just can't see it."

"As always, you're right." sighed Ben as he gave her a quick hug at the end of her driveway. "See you in the morning."

The boy rode the last two blocks home with renewed energy. Sam was right. He would avoid Greg and not fall into his scheme.

Anatomy class the next day was spent as it had been for the last few weeks. Mr. Scott lectured, and Ben tried to focus in between glances at his angel.

The hour-long torture ended with the ringing bell and all the students seemed to arrive at the narrow door simultaneously. As Ben worked his way through the opening, Lily's long blonde, silky hair brushed his face leaving the faint aroma of her perfume to entice his nostrils.

Always and Forever

Electrified, Ben made his way down the crowded hallway solely focused on Greg's letterman's jacket. Barely breaking stride, he looked firmly at the smiling quarterback. "Friday. I'll have the tests for you at lunch on Friday."

Guilt ripped Ben's heart over the next couple of days and most of Thursday night was spent staring at his bedroom ceiling. But each time he thought of abandoning his plan, he would see the beautiful face in his mind. It was with firm resolve that he sat the brown folder in front of Greg at lunch Friday.

"Welcome to the real world, Ben," Greg said calmly as he glanced into the folder. "Here's my pink slip as promised, but I'm sure you'll be returning it by Monday. Come by my house tonight at eight and I'll introduce you to a man that can make all your dreams and desires come true. 330 Pine Street."

Ben was puzzled, but took the pink slip and replied, "Eight o'clock, 330 Pine; I'll be there."

Throughout the rest of the day, Ben walked around with a gnawing feeling deep in the pit of his stomach. It was as if something had left him, leaving a sense of foreboding he couldn't explain.

The feeling was so unsettling that Ben signed out at the start of his last class and pedaled home alone.

At eight o'clock, he found himself riding his bicycle up to 330 Pine Street. Greg's house was a much newer, large white ranch with a bright red door that seemed to glow under the fluorescent streetlight. The Firebird was the only car in the drive, and a single light shone through the window.

Greg opened the red door as Ben made his way cautiously up the walk. "Come on in, buddy. Are you ready to have Lily all to yourself?"

Ben smiled weakly and nodded as he walked through the open door.

It felt like a trap, and the emptiness inside of Ben had grown from discomfort to real physical pain, but he had to take the chance - for her. The vision of her face and smell of that sweet perfume kept driving him forward and into the living room where he found a dark-haired man sitting in the rocking chair.

The man was impeccably dressed in a black suit with a bright red shirt and black silk tie. His beard was short and carefully shaped to a small narrow point. It was accentuated by a thin mustache. His complexion was smooth and very pale, contrasting his hair and dark eyes.

"You must be Ben," the gentleman said in a mild but jovial tone. "I am Mr. Lucifer and am very pleased to meet you." The man reached out and grasped Ben's hand in a firm handshake.

Every fiber of Ben's being told him to turn and run. To run fast and hard and stop for nothing; but as Ben began to pull away, Mr. Lucifer spoke again. "Greg tells me you are very interested in a beautiful girl named Lily. Sit, and let's see what we can do to help you win her heart."

With the mention of Lily's name, Ben fought his desire to run and found a seat on the sofa across from Mr. Lucifer.

"I am a busy man, Ben, and don't have time to toy around with the situation. So, I will cut to the chase. I am prepared to give you Lily's heart. She will love you and be totally committed to you, and none other, forever."

"That is preposterous! How can you do that? How can you make such promises?" said Ben, realizing how impossible the prospect was.

"Let's just say that I have some influence over Lily's decisions. I'll guarantee these things and only require your signature on this contract."

"A contract? What kind of contract?"

Always and Forever

"A simple one. A contract that guarantees that I'll deliver all that I have promised. If I fail to deliver, then the contract is void."

"What's my end of the bargain?"

"Come, come, Ben; surely, you're not this naïve. You get to live out your life with Lily by your side; to enjoy every moment with her, and to have your friends stare in envy as the two of you walk arm in arm. You can have all this, and more, by agreeing to give me your service after you die. You can have the woman of your dreams forever for the cost of your soul."

"My soul?!" Ben jumped to his feet and looked over to Greg and then back to Mr. Lucifer. "This is a grand joke! Mr. Lucifer…Satan…Old Scratch… I guess I really walked into this one. Are you filming this for YouTube, Greg? Are your football buddies and Lily hiding outside and watching through the windows? I'm outta here! You have the tests you wanted Greg. Just leave me alone."

As Ben turned to leave, Mr. Lucifer rose to his feet. "This isn't a joke, Ben. The contract is real, and the rewards are also very real. I have been nothing but honest with you. I hide nothing. I could have made up some phony name for myself or tried to hide what the contract demands but I have not. I am real and so is the offer, but it is a one-time offer. If you want the girl, sign it; if not, walk out, but I will not be back."

"Come on Ben," said Greg. "I'm not pulling a fast one. Sign the contract. If all this is some kind of insane joke and she is not yours by the end of the weekend, keep my car."

Ben turned back angrily and glared at the tan parchment sitting on the coffee table. "Fine! I'll finish your joke. I'll sell my soul!" He snatched the pen from the tabletop. "There, I've done it! Post your video, Greg, and you and your jerk buddies can laugh it up. But I will be driving your car."

Mr. Lucifer picked up the contract and rolled it before putting it into his jacket. "Excellent Ben," he exclaimed before reaching out to shake the boy's hand. "I'll be checking on you from time to time to see how things are progressing."

Without shaking the devil's hand, Ben stormed from the room and out the front door, leaving Lucifer and Greg behind. Lucifer pulled a second scroll from his jacket and handed it to Greg. "Our business is complete. It was nice working with you. I will miss our chats," the Devil said before vanishing.

Ben was fuming as he pedaled his bicycle hard for home. He had walked into the joke of his life and the emptiness he ignored going in was now replaced with anger.

That night, Ben's sleep was plagued with visions of little cartoon devils running about with sharp pitchforks. He tossed and turned but was rescued from his dream at dawn by his ringing cell phone.

"Hello…" Ben said sleepily.

"Hi, Ben, is that you?" asked a soft female voice. "I'm sorry to call you so early, but I need your help."

"Who is this?" asked Ben as he sat up and looked at his watch. "It's only six-thirty."

"I'm sorry. You probably don't even know who I am. I feel so foolish now. I'll let you get back to sleep. Sorry for bothering you."

"No, wait. Who are you? I'll help if I can."

"I go to school with you. I just moved into town a few weeks ago. My name's Lily Greene, but my friends call me Lil."

"Lily?" Ben asked in disbelief, now fully awake. "You're in my A/P class."

Lil giggled, "Oh good, I was afraid that you wouldn't know who I am. I never had the chance to talk with you before."

Always and Forever

Suddenly it dawned on Ben that this was part of Greg's elaborate joke and anger flashed in his voice. "Tell Greg I've had enough."

"Greg? Greg who? Oh, do you mean Greg from the football team?"

"Yeah, that Greg. Tell him the joke was very funny and that I'm very impressed a Neanderthal could come up with something so clever, but it's over."

"Ben, what are you talking about? I really don't even know Greg. I've just seen his jock-self strutting up and down the halls at school. He asked me out a few times, but he isn't my type. I got your number from Bob because he knows your little sister. I need your help getting ready for the midterms. You must be the smartest guy I've seen around school, and I am hopelessly lost. Please be a real sweetheart and help a damsel in distress."

Ben swallowed hard and took a deep breath. Maybe he would take a chance. "Can you meet me at the library when they open at ten?" he asked, wanting to set up something in a public place.

"I'd love to," cooed Lil. "I'll bring my books. You have no idea how much this means to me."

Ben said goodbye and fell back onto his pillow. "This can't be real," he whispered to himself as he looked up to the blank ceiling. Then the response reverberated through his brain, "But what if it is?" An emptiness ate away inside his stomach.

The sun sparkled off Lily's hair as she ran down the library steps to greet Ben as he rode up on his ten-speed. She almost knocked him off the seat as she threw her arms around his neck and gave him a tight squeeze. "You are such a dear to help me on your Saturday."

Thrilled by the attention and aroused by her perfume, but still skeptical, Ben looked around the area for any sign of Greg or his cretin friends. All seemed quiet as he dismounted and locked the bike to the handrail.

Lil grabbed his hand and led him up the steps and into the quiet library. The tables were empty, and the only other sign of life was Mrs. Laughlin, the librarian, checking in book returns behind the counter.

The two students sat at the far end of the room and spent the late morning and early afternoon pouring over quadratic equations and then Roman history.

Ben's phone buzzed a few times as he received texts from Sam and Pete.

"Everything okay," asked Lil as Ben replied to the texts.

"Just my friends," replied Ben. "I told them that I was helping a friend study. I'll catch up with them later."

"The dark-haired girl you sit with, in the cafeteria. She's your girlfriend?"

"Oh no," said Ben shaking his head. "We are just friends. Been so for as long as I can remember."

Lily smiled and looked back into her textbook.

As time wore on Ben became less suspicious and more comfortable when he realized he held Lily's full attention and Greg had not appeared from the shadows.

Finally, about four o'clock, she reached over and took Ben's hand, sending waves of warmth and excitement through the boy's body. "I'm so lucky to have someone as smart and sweet as you to help me study. Let's quit for today and I'll take you to the Pizza Palace and reward you for all your hard work."

"You want to be with me at the Pizza Palace? It's Saturday, everyone in town will be there."

By 'everyone' Ben meant that all the popular kids from school would be there. It was not a place he and his friends would venture to on a Saturday night.

Always and Forever

She reached over and playfully tousled his brown hair. "They have the best food in this little town and my girlfriends will be there. I want them to meet the guy that saved me from midterms. We'll even drop your bike by your house on the way, so you won't have to ride home after dark."

Ben was skeptical but decided to risk it. He stood and started packing his books while trying to watch her out of the corner of his eye. If she was setting him up for a fall, her mannerisms didn't betray her.

They left the library and took Lily's car to the Pizza Palace. As Ben expected, they found it full of teenagers. Ben hesitated at the door, but Lil grabbed his hand and pulled him through the crowd. "Come on, love, my friends are over in that booth."

Many heads turned and Ben spotted several teens laughing and pointing him out to their friends. Much of the laughing stopped as the angel and her tutor found their way to the back of the pizza parlor.

The two girls at the table seemed shocked as Lil walked up with Ben in tow. They looked even more surprised when she announced proudly that they had studied together through the day at the library and that she was hoping to persuade Ben to study more tomorrow.

The young scholar felt so out of place as he sat looking at the shocked expressions of Lil's friends, but the young girl seemed oblivious to her friend's surprised silence. Grasping Ben's hand, she announced that pizza was on her.

The pizza was good, and Ben couldn't believe how Lil kept taking his hand as they all talked; or that she kept pushing closer and closer to him. He relaxed and felt better than ever, as he listened to Lil brag to her friends about how smart and sweet he was. She finally announced that she would just have to keep him as she turned and gently kissed his cheek.

The evening went by like a whirlwind and, around midnight, she dropped him off at his home. As Ben reached for the car door handle, Lily reached over and took his left hand. "Ben?" she asked, her voice slightly quivering.

"Yes?" he replied, slightly alarmed at her sudden change in demeanor.

"I've never asked anyone this before, and well..."

"What's wrong, Lil? You can ask me anything."

The girl blushed. "I guess I'm kind of embarrassed. Embarrassed and afraid, but here goes. Can I be your girlfriend?"

"What?"

"Look, I know it sounds crazy, but I really loved spending time with you today, and, well, I can't stop thinking about you. I can understand if you don't want to, but..."

"Why wouldn't I want to? You're the most beautiful girl I've ever seen."

Tears started to swell in Lil's eyes. "You're so sweet. A big liar... but so sweet. Can I be your girlfriend then?"

"I would sell my..." started Ben as he lost himself in her blue eyes. "Oh, Lord, I've sold my soul!" thought Ben as the realization exploded in his brain. His alarm was short-lived as he lost all conscious thought when her lips touched his.

The next day at the library, Ben couldn't have been happier. The subject at hand quickly turned from studying textbooks to studying each other, and Ben finally learned more about this woman that was now his.

Lil had only started school earlier that month when she and her mother moved to Westmoreland from Colorado. Her mother was struggling to find work after Lily's father was sentenced to the penitentiary for armed robbery. None of that mattered to her now since she had found Ben.

"Armed robbery?!" thought Ben. Thoughts of violence and mayhem entered his brain. "What if he doesn't like me dating his daughter."

"Don't worry, sweetheart. Daddy will love you just as much as I do. Besides, he won't be out for quite a while."

Ben grimaced to think of what hardships his angel had endured, but each time he tried to ask more about her childhood and upbringing she changed the subject back to him. It seemed as if she had shared enough of her past and was now only interested in him. They sat locked in each other's gaze as he told her stories about his childhood and the life he spent in Westmoreland. She suddenly broke his concentration when she looked deep into his eyes and calmly announced, "You know I love you, don't you?"

Ben's heart jumped for joy. The price was hefty, but the angel was indeed his. "I've loved you since the first morning I saw you at school."

Lil dropped Ben off late at his home. He was weary as he pulled his bike from her trunk, but Lil walked up his drive with him and kissed him goodnight before leaving. Walking into the dark home, he smiled, and then painfully realized how chapped his lips had become after spending the day with his new love.

Pete and Sam were waiting at the corner as Ben came pedaling up the next morning.

"Where have you been!" shouted out the two worried friends, almost simultaneously.

Ben smiled, "You two wouldn't believe me if I told you, but you will see for yourself when we get to school."

Pete and Sam had a hard time keeping up with their eager friend as he pedaled quickly toward the High School. No sooner had they dismounted at the bike rack than Lil came running up, throwing her arms around Ben's neck.

"I missed you so much, babe," exclaimed Lil as Pete and Sam looked on, completely dumbfounded.

Not only were the two friends shocked by the completely unexpected display of affection but many of the students passing by stopped suddenly to witness the unlikely couple.

"I missed you too, Lil," smiled Ben, returning the hug. "You haven't met my two friends. Lil, this is Sam and Pete."

Lil smiled at the two friends, "You two are so lucky to have someone as smart and handsome as Ben as a friend. Sam, Ben said you and he have always been just friends, but I honestly can't see how you can keep your hands off him. Your loss though, he's all mine now." Then looking back to Ben added, "Right Lover?"

"All yours," confirmed Ben. "You better get to your first class. I'll catch up to you later in Anatomy."

Lil smiled and blew him a kiss as she hurried off to class.

"What the hell was that?!" loudly exclaimed Pete as Lil vanished into the crowd.

Ben smiled broadly and shrugged his shoulders. "I helped her study Saturday and Sunday. I guess she couldn't resist my charm."

"What charm?" scowled Sam. "Honestly guys, either I'm dreaming, or this is some scene from the Twilight Zone. Pete, you don't see something terribly wrong here?"

"Hey, if I was Ben and she thought I had charm, well, who am I to argue?" smiled Pete as he punched his buddy in the shoulder. "Go

Always and Forever

with it while you can. Who knows how long it will be before she sees the eye doctor and gets glasses."

Sam exhaled sharply and looked at Ben. "If you're happy then that's what matters. I just don't want to see you get hurt or ruin your future."

Ben was about to voice his reassurance but suddenly remembered. "Class! We need to get to class."

The fourth period found Lil and Ben in their assigned seats but Ben's glances at his angel were now returned, and the boy couldn't be happier.

Life was good and Ben knew he would have to return Greg's pink slip at lunch. It hadn't been a joke after all. Lil was now his. He forced himself not to think of the cost. He would have his heaven on Earth now instead of thinking about a final reward later.

Midterm exams came and went, but Ben found it difficult to do as well as he would have liked. His thoughts were full of love and stolen kisses at the lockers. Lil filled his days and evenings. She was always there between classes and waiting at his locker at the final bell. She had abandoned her friends and only had eyes and time for her new man.

Pete was unlocking his bike as Sam approached with her canvas book bag. Ben was now driven to and from school by Lil.

"Hey Sam," greeted the lanky lad. "I kinda miss riding home with ol' Ben. I thought things would have slowed down a little between the two lovebirds."

Sam frowned. "Not a chance. Did you see how he did on his midterms? If he doesn't pull out of this nosedive, he can kiss med school goodbye."

"It might be time for some tough love. An intervention! Meet me at Ben's tonight at 10. Maybe we can get through to him."

Right at 10 the duo knocked on Ben's front door. After a moment the door slowly opened, and Ben's mom looked out at the two friends.

"Samantha! Pete! What's wrong? It's 10 o'clock."

"I'm sorry. I know it's late, but we needed to talk with Ben for just a few minutes."

"Well, he hasn't walked in yet but should any minute. That new girlfriend of his keeps him as long as she can. I finally was able to get him home on school nights by 10. To them, that means 5 or 10 minutes after, but I'll take it."

"She's what we need to talk to him about. His grades are slipping, and we are worried," confessed Pete.

"You two are good friends." smiled the mom. "I know she makes him happy, but he needs to get his priorities straight. No reason he can't have her in his life and study too."

The two friends nodded.

"Go on to his room. He always comes in, grabs a coke, and heads for bed."

"Thanks," said Sam as she and Pete entered the house.

As anticipated, Lily's car arrived a few minutes later and after a lengthy kiss goodnight, Ben was sprinting up the walk to his front door.

True to his habits, Ben grabbed a cold Coke from the fridge and headed down the hallway, humming a lively Aerosmith song. The tune abruptly stopped as he walked in a found his two friends waiting.

"Hey guys," greeted Ben cautiously. "Is something wrong?"

Always and Forever

"You could say that," said Sam with concern. "What is happening to you? I have seen some of the grades you have been getting lately. You don't study. You don't focus in class. Yeah, Ben, something is wrong."

Ben's smile vanished as he sat on the edge of the bed. "Aw, come on, Sam. Sure, I have been a little less driven lately, but it isn't that bad."

Pete shook his head. "I got a better grade on my AP exam today. I'm no dummy but I can't remember you ever bombing a test like that. Sam's right. Your head is definitely somewhere other than school."

Still sitting on the end of the bed, Ben just looked at the ground for several long moments. "You really beat me on that exam?" he grimaced. "I just thought the test was harder for everyone."

"Come on Ben," said Sam. "We have been in the same classes since kindergarten. You have had your future planned out since the 6th grade. Remember when you decided to be a doctor and not a rodeo clown?"

Ben chuckled, "I do remember. I guess I have been a little preoccupied with Lily lately. I never had a real girlfriend before, and it has only been a few weeks."

"Nobody is suggesting you lose the girlfriend," said Pete. "You just need to get a few nights each week to hit the books."

Ben smiled, "Yeah, Lily and I have tried a few times to study together at her house, but we always get to kissing after about 15 minutes and the next thing I know it's almost 10 o'clock."

"You're making out with her mom at home? You dog!" exclaimed Pete with a big smile.

Ben returned the smile, "No her mom is always working. It's kinda rough on Lily but you are both right. I need a night or two to get in some studies."

"More like two or three," said Sam, obviously not as impressed as Pete had been. "Even four wouldn't hurt. Graduation is only a few months away and acceptance letters could be coming soon."

"I'll study tomorrow night," announced Ben firmly. You both can join me here if you want."

The two friends readily agreed and left for home, happy that the intervention had been well received.

Lily was all smiles as she picked up Ben for school the next morning, but the smile quickly faded after her beau mentioned studying with Pete and Sam after school. After a tense moment of silence, the smile returned. "Great!" she replied enthusiastically, "I barely know your friends. It will be fun for the four of us to study. Well, maybe not as much fun as our study sessions but we are bound to get more studying done."

Ben swallowed hard but forced a smile. The prospect was unsettling but what could go wrong? "Sounds good, sweetheart. We are all meeting at my house after school."

The smile vanished from Sam's face as she and Pete walked into Ben's room to find Lily sitting next to Ben at his desk.

"Hey guys!" exclaimed Lily, wearing a grin that would put the Cheshire Cat to shame. "Ben said we are all meeting for a study session."

Pete felt a little uncomfortable as he looked at Lily and then back to Sam. "The more the merrier," offered Pete, trying to ease the tension.

"I guess," said Sam, trying to force a smile and not appear that she was doing so. "We should probably work on Anatomy since it is the only class we all four have together."

Always and Forever

Lil giggled, "Maybe you two should go on home and I'll help Ben study some anatomy."

Blushing, Ben quickly spoke up to divert attention from Lil's flirtation. "Yeah, we have that test on cellular respiration and division next week. This could be a good chance to bump our grades up."

Time pressed on slowly, but every time headway was made Lily would tousle Ben's hair or say something to distract him from the work at hand. The last straw snapped when, from out of the blue, Lily exclaimed, "You know, Pete, you and Sam make a really cute couple."

Pete looked up from his textbook and stared at Lily in silence while Sam glared at Ben.

Fearing impending war, Ben jumped in. "Well, I don't know about everyone else, but I think my brain's about to explode. Maybe we should call it a night."

Pete's book was closed before Ben could finish the sentence and within a minute Sam and Pete slipped out the door leaving Ben and Lily in the room.

"You didn't say anything about Pete and Sam, lover," said Lily. "Don't you agree about them as a couple?"

"I don't know sweetheart. I just can't see Sam and Pete even holding hands."

A darkness fell across the angel's face and her voice became stern, "I don't see why you wouldn't want Sam with Pete. Does the thought make you jealous? You want Sam for yourself, don't you?"

Ben was dumbfounded and stared blankly at Lily. This was a Lily he didn't know, and he began to stammer as he searched for words.

Lily stomped her foot down. "I can't believe it. You want Sam for yourself!"

"Wait, wait, wait!" pleaded Ben. "Sweetheart! Sam is just a friend. I love you."

Lily's expression shifted again. "You aren't interested in Sam?"

"No! Not at all. She is like my sister." Ben looked a little sick as he said it. "Dating my sister would be gross."

Giggling and smiling, as if nothing had happened, she kissed Ben's cheek. "Well, I guess I'll forgive you this time. But remember, you're all mine. See you tomorrow."

Before he could blink, Ben found himself standing alone in his room wondering what had just happened.

Sleep eluded Ben for several hours as the completely unexpected end to the study session played itself over and over in his troubled mind.

Over the last several weeks he had realized Lily had become a little possessive, but the flare of anger and jealousy chilled him to the bone.

Since he had been dating Lily, he had become popular in school. The guys were envious and looked at Ben with new respect and admiration. Many wanted to call him 'friend' in hopes his aura of popularity would enhance their attractiveness. The girls, on the other hand, wondered what it was about Ben that would attract the most beautiful girl in school, and keep her under his spell week after week.

A few times, Ben could see Lil glare at some unfortunate girl who had let her interests show in her presence. Ben even overheard one boy refer to him as being kept on a short leash.

Truth be told, Lily did keep him close, and Ben rarely found himself alone at his locker or between classes. He accepted all this as Lil being overly protective of her boyfriend and even welcomed the attention. After all, the self-proclaimed geek had never been thought of as popular, and had never had a girlfriend, let alone, an angel demanding his attention.

This night, however, was different. Lily had never been angry with him or accused him of wanting someone else. The look that had come over her face, the anger in her eyes, this scared him a little and for the first time, he found himself questioning his desires and his deal with Satan.

Finally, he rationalized that Lily had been overly tired and out of her element in the study session. Smiling, Ben naively decided that in the future he would either study with Sam and Pete or with Lil. He just couldn't study with them all at the same time.

Jumping up at the sound of the alarm, Ben was ready for school and waiting for Lily to pick him up in record time. He was so happy to see Lil's smiling angelic face as she pulled up to his house.

"Hey lover," she called out happily, "need a ride?"

Relieved, Ben returned the smile and jumped into the car. "I'll go anywhere with you."

Between periods, Pete was able to catch up with Ben during one of the few minutes he was alone.

"Dude! What kinda crap was that last night? Pushing the idea of me and Sam dating?"

"I know, Pete. I'm sorry but you should have seen what happened after you left. We can't study like that again."

"You're right about that! I think I'm just going to stay clear of your girlfriend if she intends on playing matchmaker. I like Sam and all, but it would be really weird. Too weird."

"Let's just say I never saw Lil as the jealous type, but she kinda scared me. We're all good now but…"

Just as Ben was about to finish, Pete saw Lily approaching from behind.

"Hey Lily!" exclaimed Pete, just in time to save his friend.

"Hi Pete," replied Lily in a cheerful voice. "I didn't mean to interrupt. You two boys finish talking. I just wanted a quick hug before class."

"Oh," stammered Ben, "Pete was just telling me he needed help with his calculus class and wanted me to come over after school."

Lily made a horrified face, "Calculus? Ugh. I can't stand the thought. I was lucky to pass algebra. Just thinking I would even think about calculus would make my head hurt."

"So, you wouldn't mind my giving him a hand for an hour or so this afternoon?"

"Don't be silly, lover, as long as I get you back afterward. I thought we could grab a pizza tonight."

Ben smiled, "Pizza sounds great. We'll be done by five."

"Gotta run. See you after five then, lover. You two don't study too hard."

Lily kissed Ben's cheek and started off. After a couple of steps, she glanced back. "Is Sam going to be studying with you too?"

Ben smiled, "No angel. It will just be us."

Satisfied, Lily darted off leaving Pete staring at Ben.

"Calculus? I am good at calculus. Why did you tell her that?"

"Sorry, Pete. I do need the study time and just can't do it with her there. Can you and Sam meet me at your house right after school?"

"But why did you tell her Sam wouldn't be there if you want me to tell Sam to come over?"

"It's a long story buddy but I'll fill you in this afternoon."

Always and Forever

Pete frowned, "Why didn't you just tell her the truth? You can study and have a girlfriend at the same time. You do have a life apart from Lily."

"I know. But, trust me, this is just easier. So, we're good?"

"Fine with me, but I'll ask Sam next period. Catch you after school."

Ben smiled and watched his friend disappear into the crowded hallway.

Later that afternoon, Lily dropped Ben off at home.

"Want me to pick you up at Pete's at 5:00, lover?"

Ben shook his head, "No baby. I may get done earlier and just head over to your house then. I'm looking forward to a hot pepperoni pizza and a certain hot girlfriend."

With a quick kiss, Ben turned and trotted off to the house as Lily drove off.

After a needed snack Ben was on his bicycle and headed toward Pete's.

Sam was already cracking the books with Pete when Ben came walking into the bedroom with a big smile. "Hey guys, let's hit it."

As the twilight greeted the oncoming night, Lily became bored and drove the neighborhood hoping to see Ben on his way. Passing Pete's house, she noticed Ben's bike still outside and became alarmed to see Sam's bike sitting there too. Lily drove around the corner and parked out of sight.

She walked down the sidewalk and approached Pete's home in the dark yard. The three friends were just wrapping up and Pete slipped out of the room for a moment just as Lily peered through his bedroom window on her tippy toes. Her blue eyes grew wide as she looked in and saw Ben and Sam alone in Pete's room.

"That Bitch!" she whispered as she backed away from the window. "She is trying to steal my poor Ben."

Lily was waiting outside her home as Ben arrived on his bike. The angel gave Ben a huge hug and kiss. "Ready for pizza, lover?"

The night went well and the subject of school or studying never came up. Later, Lily dropped Ben off at his home and gave him a deep kiss goodnight.

"I love you so much," said Lily almost sounding desperate.

"I love you too, baby," whispered Ben.

"I don't know what I would ever do if I lost you. I can't stand the thought."

"Oh baby, you don't ever have to worry about that. I'll see you tomorrow morning."

Lily smiled, but as she drove off, the smile quickly vanished.

Ben became a little worried the next day, as Lily was absent from Mr. Scott's class. She had driven him to school, and he had seen her a few times before the Anatomy class but now she was a no-show. His fears were relieved as he walked out into the parking lot after school and saw Lily waiting by her car.

"I missed you, baby. Where were you?"

"Sorry love, I had an errand to run. If you kept your phone on you could have called me."

Ben smiled, "I guess, but…"

"But nothing, love. Here, I got you something." Lily proudly held out a box for Ben.

"A smartwatch? You bought me a smartwatch?"

Always and Forever

The huge smile and nodding head answered any question. "Keep your phone in your backpack and wear the watch. Now we can get in touch with each other, so much easier."

"Wow!" exclaimed Ben with noted hesitation. "I don't know what to say."

Lil giggled. "I think a big kiss and then maybe you could just whisper 'thank you' in my ear before you grab a quick nibble."

Ben smiled broadly. "Okay, I think I can do just that."

Later that evening, the lovebirds took in a movie and pulled up to Ben's house at about 9:00.

"Sorry, I'm dropping you off early, but I've had a little bit of a rough day. A girl has to get her beauty sleep."

Ben laughed out loud, "That's one thing you don't need, gorgeous. It is not possible for anyone to be more beautiful than you."

Lily gave him a big squeeze. "You are such a liar," she giggled. "See you in the morning."

Walking down the hall toward his room, Ben wondered what he would do with his free time. Startled by the vibration on his wrist, it took a second for him to realize it was his new watch.

"Hello?" he said cautiously.

"You are so silly," laughed Lily. "It's like you have never answered a phone."

"Sorry, I guess I just never answered my phone on my wrist."

"Fair enough, Lover. I was just calling to check on you. Miss me yet?"

"I do. Are you sure you need to rest? You could come back over."

"Now don't be a crybaby. I'll see you in the morning. Still love me?"

"More than ever. Goodnight angel."

The phone disconnected as Ben sat at his desk and decided to get a little studying in before bed.

Sam was studying quietly in her room enjoying the warm spring breeze from her open window when she was surprised to see Lily peeking in from outside and waving to get her attention.

The nerdy girl walked over to the window. "Hi Lily, is everything alright?"

"Oh, I'm fine, everything's okay. Sorry to startle you but I want to do something for Ben, and I think you know him better than anyone. Tomorrow is Friday; can you meet me about 9 tomorrow night?"

"I guess," replied Sam, a little surprised and a little proud that Lily would come to her.

"I know you don't ever go to the pizzeria, but we could meet at the library about nine. It's quieter there and on Friday they don't close until 10:00. I can even give you a ride home after we talk."

"Alright, I'll meet you there at 9," said Sam with a warm smile. "I take it this will be a surprise for Ben, so I won't mention our meeting to anyone."

"You are a saint," exclaimed Lily. "I'll see you then."

Lily turned and trotted off, her blonde hair disappearing into the dark night. Smiling broadly, she jumped into her car and sped off into the cool night air but didn't go directly home.

Parking away from the streetlamps, Lily walked quietly down the street while putting on a pair of leather gloves. After turning down an alley, she passed two houses and then slipped into the backyard of the third. All was quiet in the dark backyard and Lily crept to the wooden tool shed and tried the doorknob.

The angel was pleased with her luck as she found the doorknob turn easily in her hand. The door opened quietly and peering in with a small flashlight, she selected a shovel. Turning back towards the door, she spied an old used mower blade hanging on a rusty forgotten nail.

"Perfect!" whispered Lily as she removed the mower blade from the nail and slipped out of the storage shed, closing the door quietly behind her.

Creeping to the back of the shed she hid the mower blade in the blooming daffodils that were making their early spring appearance.

The contented blonde returned to her car with the shovel and, placing a plastic shopping bag over the shovel blade, she put it into her spacious trunk.

The unsuspecting neighborhood continued to sleep quietly as she drove off into the night.

Morning came and was no different than the previous one, or the one before that. The school year was getting close to graduation and seniors would be ordering caps and gowns in the next two weeks for Spring graduation just a few months away.

Soon after the final bell, Ben's phone buzzed, and Lily texted that she was waiting at the car.

"On my way," texted Ben as he trotted past the lockers. He was surprised to see Lily frowning as he got to the car. "What's wrong Angel?"

"It's my friend Kitty. She heard at lunch that her boyfriend was seeing somebody else. It was quite a fight. Of course, he lied and said it wasn't true, but Kitty is heartbroken. I need to stay over at her house tonight and help her get over this. You know, we can sit and talk about how 'lowlife, cheating liars' some of you boys are."

Ben was disappointed. This would be their first Friday night apart since they started dating. Trying to be supportive he shrugged his shoulders and smiled weakly. "I understand. We will have lots of Friday nights together. Help her out tonight, and maybe we can spend some time together tomorrow. Just don't include me in your talk about lowlife boys."

"I don't know if I've told you this before, but you are the best! I knew you would understand." She gave him a big kiss and the two drove off to Ben's house.

Lily was waiting in the back of the parking lot at the library when Sam came riding up at 9. The car had been backed into a spot with its taillights facing the wooded lot next to the library.

"Hey Lily," said Sam as she stopped her bicycle. "I almost didn't see you over here. It's a little dark."

"Sorry, some cars have been getting damaged lately, and I thought over here would be too out of the way for people to mess with."

Lily opened her trunk. "Here, we can put your bike in now, so we can just leave when we're done talking."

"Good idea," agreed Sam, as she walked the bike over and started to place it into the empty spacious trunk.

"Thank goodness there is lots of room. You even have plastic over your carpet to keep it clean," observed Sam, as she leaned over the trunk and settled her bike on the stiff plastic.

"You are right about that!" said Lily as she brought the shovel down hard onto the back of Sam's head.

Sam momentarily felt the intense pain of the shovel blow before all went dark. The girl's limp body was tossed on top of her bike. Looking around, and content that she was alone, Lily took off the gloves, tossed them and the shovel on top of Sam, and closed the trunk.

Lily calmly drove to Kitty's house a few miles away, retrieved her cell phone from Kitty's mailbox, and raised it to her ear.

"Hey lover," she sighed as Ben answered the phone.

"Hey Lil, how are things going?"

"Even better than expected," said Lily brightly. "I'm going to stay here tonight and catch up to you in the morning."

"Alright babe, sleep tight."

"You too, lover. Dream about me!"

The phone clicked in Ben's ear as he was about to respond. Closing his textbook, he decided to get some sleep.

Lily knocked on the door and a puffy-eyed Kitty answered. "Oh good, you did come," she said brightly.

"I told you I would. I even brought you something to help you sleep. Now let's think about getting you a new boyfriend."

Kitty found a weak smile as she and Lily walked to her bedroom.

About half an hour after taking the pill Lily had brought, Kitty found it impossible to keep her eyes open. Ensuring Kitty was out cold, Lily silenced her phone and left it on the dresser before opening the bedroom window and slipping out into the darkness of night.

Driving down the dark road Lily could hear stirring and soft moaning coming from the trunk of the car. "Good," she thought out loud. "The little Princess is awake. I thought I would have to drag her boyfriend-stealing ass across the ground."

She pulled the car into a dark playground and turned the lights and engine off. All was peaceful and dark as the deserted monkey bars and swings rested under the bright stars ready for the next morning's invasion by laughing, running children.

Lily opened the trunk and grabbed Sam by her blood-soaked hair before pulling hard to drag her dazed and aching body out of the trunk. "Come on bitch. It's two in the morning and I want to get back and get my beauty sleep," snarled Lily as Sam fell from the trunk.

"What are you doing?" cried Sam, as she tried to get to her unsteady feet.

"Teaching you to stay away from Ben."

"What are you talking about? I don't want Ben. He is just a friend."

Lily reached into the trunk and then, with her other hand, grabbed Sam again by her hair, pulling her away from the car and to a nearby picnic table.

"Why wouldn't you want Ben? You think you're too good for him?" she snarled again, twisting Sam's words, and throwing her against the hardwood of the picnic table.

Sam cried out in pain and fell to the ground. "Lily, don't do this! Ben is yours. Let me go. I won't tell anyone about this." The terrified girl tried desperately to crawl away and get to her feet to run, but Lily stepped hard on her back and shoved her forcefully to the ground.

"No, you don't, bitch! I'm not ready to let you go."

Sam began crying, the tears cascading down her dirty face and past her trembling lips. "Please Lily, please. Don't hurt me anymore. Please let me go. I won't tell anyone. I promise I won't tell."

Lily reached down and grabbed Sam by the front of her shirt lifting her to her feet. The enraged blonde pulled Sam's face closer and looked into her wet tear-filled brown eyes, illuminated only by the moonlight. "You will stay away from Ben?" she growled.

"I swear I will. I swear! Ben is all yours. You are right. I am not good enough for him."

"You're damn right you will," hissed Lily through gritted teeth as she raised the mower blade and brought it down hard onto Sam's head.

The sickening sound of breaking skull rang out as the mower blade sank deep into the brunette's brain with a splatter of blood and pink soft brain tissue. Sam's knees immediately buckled, and her right arm and shoulder convulsed and twitched as she hit the ground. The girl's eyes stared up at the stars in the black velvet sky as her mouth silently opened and closed several times as she involuntarily gasped for air.

Looking down at the dying teen, Lily felt nothing but burning rage. "Why don't you die already?" she spat as she smiled and brought the mower blade down again and again on Sam's mangled head, leaving bits of white bone and brain scattered on the dark grass, glistening and almost glowing in the moonlight.

In her jealousy-fueled, bloodlust, and insane frenzy, Lily hacked away with the mower blade working to dismember the corpse. The dull edge tore at the flesh more than cut it and Lily's arm began to tire, her breathing labored. Cursing herself, she made a promise to find a sharper blade next time. Looking at the car she remembered the shovel and decided its blade might be sharper and work better. Soon, piece by piece, she carried Sam to the nearby dumpster and tossed her in.

Now, she needed to remove any evidence that could implicate her. Ben would need her more than ever now that his friend was gone. Now was her time.

Returning to the car, she retrieved Sam's bike and carefully removed the plastic from the floor of the trunk. The blood on the plastic had begun to dry and left nothing behind to be found. The bike was left against the picnic table and the plastic was wadded up and placed in the barbeque pit next to the table.

Smiling, the murderess removed her gloves and the size 11 boy's sneakers she had been wearing like oversized clown shoes. She then stripped off all her bloodied clothes and put everything carefully on top of the wadded plastic and, standing naked in the moonlight, she lit the plastic on fire. Grabbing the blade with a plastic grocery bag, she turned and picked up a second dark object from the ground. "Can't forget this," she giggled.

Moving quickly, she made her way to the bathroom in the center of the park and washed herself at the outside faucet. Still wet, she jumped into her car and pulled quietly away without her lights, into the dark street.

Only a little over a block away, she left the car and crept up an alleyway to a familiar shed. She quietly returned the rusty, dull mower blade and shovel to their places and closed the door. She went to the back of the shed and shoved the old plastic shopping bag under the raised back of the shed.

The evil angel looked up to the sky and smiled. "All done," she whispered as she brushed any dirt from her hands. "Now to go and get a little sleep. My Ben will need me."

Dry and in fresh clothes, Lily slipped into Kitty's open window and returned to bed. Content, she slipped off to sleep listening to her friend's soft snoring.

Loud sirens broke the still Saturday morning air before the dew could completely dry from the green spring grass. Police cars sped through the waking streets as they converged on the family park. Several horrified parents clutching their children watched with relief as the officers arrived.

Always and Forever

The early morning's relaxing cup of coffee, while watching the children play, was shattered, when one of the youngsters, running across the park, slipped and fell in a pool of fresh blood.

The hysterically screaming woman on the 911 call was the most excitement this town had seen in several years and pulses were racing as the officers jumped from their cruisers.

Soon, statements were taken, and the entire park was cordoned off with bright yellow crime scene tape as detectives descended onto the park. The entire area was a beehive of activity. Unfortunately, the excited police officers of the Westmoreland PD seemed frazzled and ill-prepared for the task at hand.

The town was usually quiet and there hadn't been a homicide in over four years. The Police Department didn't even have a dedicated homicide department or detective. Detectives from the robbery division were tasked to oversee any homicides that may occur.

The chief of police showed up around an hour after the first officers had arrived on the scene.

"What do you make of this Bob?" asked the puzzled chief.

"Not sure boss," replied a detective in a black polo shirt and khaki trousers. "The Campbell woman discovered a lot of blood over by the picnic table. I looked over at the area and found footprints tracking through the blood and I think pieces of bone."

"Is there a body?"

"No chief. Not sure yet what might have happened here, but it doesn't look too good for someone."

"What about the bike over there by the table?"

The detective scratched his head and looked over at the bicycle. "It was here when Mrs. Campbell and her little girl arrived."

Just then, a younger detective yelled out, as he dropped the heavy metal lid on the dumpster and vomited, clutching his stomach.

The chief jerked his head up at the sound of the commotion. "John, you dumbass, don't you throw up on my crime scene." He then yelled out to all the officers, "Everyone! Stop what you are doing and leave the park by the shortest path. John! Pull yourself together and meet me at my car."

Just then, the chief's cell phone rang. "Damn! What now?" grumbled the chief aloud as he pulled the phone from his shirt pocket. Glancing at the caller ID he saw that it was dispatch calling.

"What Margie? What? I am kinda busy here."

"Sorry Chief," replied the voice. "I just got a call from your daughter. Sam didn't come home last night."

The chief's gaze again fixed on the bicycle standing silently ownerless against the picnic table. His mouth moved slowly but no words escaped as all the color drained from his weathered face and his knees gave way. His cherished Sam. No please, not his Sam.

Ben was just starting to stir when his mother knocked loudly on his bedroom door. "Ben, Ben! Get dressed and come to the living room. The police are here."

Ben's mind cleared instantly at the word 'police'. The boy sprang from bed, into his jeans, and was pulling his shirt over his head as he exploded through his doorway and into the hallway.

The detective and two uniformed officers turned abruptly as Ben bolted into the room.

"Is Lily alright?" said the alarmed youth a little louder than he had intended.

"Lily? Who is Lily?" asked the detective calmly as he glanced at his notepad.

Always and Forever

"Oh, that's Bennie's new girlfriend," volunteered the mother.

"Mom!" exclaimed Ben visibly annoyed. The boy then turned to the detective. "She is my girlfriend. Is she okay?"

"I couldn't say, son. We are just here to ask you a few questions about Samantha Reynolds. You have been her friend for a long time."

"They met in kindergarten," confirmed Ben's mom.

"Mrs. Strong, you are more than welcome to be present while we talk to Ben, but we really need to speak with just him."

Mrs. Strong's face became pale as she began to realize the seriousness of this conversation. "Should we have a lawyer present?"

The detective tried his best to give a reassuring and disarming smile. "No ma'am, nothing like that."

Ben finally found an opportunity to jump into the conversation. "Sam? Why are you asking me about Sam?"

The smile vanished from the detective's face. "When did you last see Sam?"

"Yesterday at school. Is she missing? What is going on?!" demanded Ben, becoming very alarmed.

One of the uniformed officers placed a hand on Ben's shoulder. "Something bad has happened, Ben. Really bad."

Tears were streaming down Ben's cheeks as he pedaled madly towards Pete's house. Never in his young life had the boy felt the churning chaos of feelings trapped inside his chest. How was it possible to feel empty and numb at the same time he felt his chest was about to explode?

After answering the detective's questions, all Ben could think about was getting to Pete. The boy had no idea why or what Pete could do to help but he needed his friend. He pedaled so hard and was so focused that Ben never even noticed the unmarked police car following him.

A patrol car was pulling away from Pete's house as Ben whipped his bike into the driveway. Pete was standing on the porch watching the car when Ben ran up and threw his arms around his friend. The two boys just stood for several minutes crying about the loss of their best friend.

Finally, the anger escaped, and Ben wiped his eyes. "What the hell happened?! Who could ever hurt Sam?"

Pete was defeated. "I don't know, Ben. Everyone loved Sam. Everyone. If someone could hurt Sam, then are we in danger too?"

Ben shrugged.

"What about Lily? Does she know?"

"Damn! I forgot all about Lily. I have to call her."

After a few rings, Lily picked up. "Angel, are you alright? Something bad has happened. Please, get over to Pete's house as quickly as you can. No Lil, I'm okay. I'll tell you everything when you get here. Please hurry!"

Lily arrived and the three friends sat in the living room at Pete's. Ben was in rough shape and Pete was doing all he could to console his friend, but Lily was deeply annoyed. She was supposed to be the one comforting Ben. Every time she was able to get Ben to rest his head on her shoulder, Pete would say something, and Ben would move. Finally, after about an hour or so, she was able to get Ben to agree to go for a ride to clear his head.

The State Investigators began pouring into the small town at about noon. Ben and Lily were sitting in her car at the library as the marked trooper's cars drove past.

"Don't worry, love. I just know they will catch the guy that did this."

Always and Forever

Ben watched the patrol cars for a moment and then looked back to Lily. Even now the young man's face was puffy and his eyes red and swollen. "I sure hope so. What kind of insane freak would do something so…so vile?"

Lilly felt a little angry and defensive about the 'insane freak' conclusion but tried hard to remain calm for her Ben. "Maybe he isn't insane at all. Maybe something else motivated it. Hate or maybe even love."

"Love? You gotta be kidding me!"

"A powerful emotion," defended Lily. "More crimes have been committed and lives lost in the name of love than anything else. Think of Romeo and Juliet, or Anthony and Cleopatra."

Ben shrugged. "I still can't think of anyone that knew Sam as being capable of such violence."

"Try not to think of it, I'll take care of you," smiled Lily as she took Ben's hand and squeezed tightly.

The blocks around the park were sealed off as the state's forensic team poured over the crime scene. News trucks and reporters from nearby cities tried desperately to get a little bit closer than their competitors. The whole town was now buzzing with the news and theories ran wild from a secret jealous boyfriend to a satanic ritual. A few of the more free-thinking individuals believed aliens from space were conducting experiments. Boyfriend or aliens, most folks were scared, and kids were kept inside.

Activity at the park slowed as the sun began to set. Doors and windows were locked and double-checked for protection from the unknown. The entire dumpster containing Sam's remains was sent to the crime lab for forensic pathologists to comb over. Hundreds of pictures had been taken and the grounds had been searched literally inch by inch for any possible clues. All had taken place as the chief stood silently by, watching.

A state investigator had approached the chief earlier in the day and commented on how badly the crime scene had been compromised. "Your men really botched this up, chief. I hope we can find something they haven't walked all over that will give us a clue about who chopped up the kid."

The stoic police chief silently turned red and lunged at the state investigator, grabbing his collar. Two of the chief's lieutenants grabbed the chief and pulled him away. One led the chief towards a squad car while the other stayed behind.

"The 'kid' was his only grandchild," scolded the lieutenant as he also began to walk away. "Guess you missed that point in the arrival briefing, asshole."

The few remaining investigators wrapped up their work in the wee hours of the morning. Crime barriers were removed by sunrise and the park reopened but stayed deserted. People walking by did so on the other side of the street and did so quickly as if they were children avoiding a haunted house on Halloween.

The schools announced they would be closed all week and police patrolled the area heavily in car and on foot searching for anyone that looked out of place. The advantage of a small town is knowing your neighbors, and any outsider was scrutinized heavily.

Lily wouldn't let Ben out of her sight and the constant comforting was starting to wear on his nerves. Monday afternoon, as they were driving to Ben's house, he told Lily that he needed her to drop him off at Pete's house. "I just need to check on Pete and see how he is holding up."

"Okay, lover, we can check on him together. I worry about him too."

"Oh, I know you do but I don't want you getting home and locked safely inside too late. They haven't caught that killer yet."

"No. I don't mind. I don't want you getting home too late either."

"Not to worry. If it gets too late, I'll just crash at Pete's and see you in the morning. I'll call my folks. I'm sure they will be fine with it."

A flash of anger crossed the girl's face but was quickly replaced with a smile.

"Sure, lover, whatever you want."

After a few days, anxiety in the Westmoreland began to die down as many folks assumed the killer must be long gone. They just couldn't bring themselves to believe someone that depraved could live among them.

The chief had wisely put himself on paid leave and left the case to his lead detective, Chandler Farmer, a tall, slender, young blonde go-getter, citing a conflict of interest. Unfortunately, Chandler was coming up empty-handed in his interviews with Ben and Pete. He had even met with Lily in hopes of shedding some light on Sam and her activities that fateful night.

Three days after the murder, Farmer made the 3-hour drive to the state crime lab for a briefing on the autopsy and evidence findings. Walking into the medical examiner's office, he was greeted by a surprisingly pleasant younger man seated behind a desk piled high with charts, folders, and photographs.

"Hi Detective," the doctor said calmly while standing up and extending his right hand. "I'm Doctor Kernek. I have finished up and signed the autopsy findings on your murdered girl, Samantha."

The pathologist lowered himself back to his seat and picked up a folder as Chandler sat across from him. "It is no surprise, but I have officially ruled the death a homicide. That was without any question. The poor girl died as a result of head trauma. It looked to be a blunt force with a narrow metal object. I did find traces of rust embedded in the wound edges, so whatever it was, is older, ferrous metal and has a rusty blunted edge."

"Ferrous?"

"Contains iron. Steel, cast iron, anything attracted by a magnet."

Chandler looked up from taking notes. "A crowbar, perhaps?"

"I don't think so. It would be too wide. You are looking for something like an old, very dull machete."

"Do you think the death blow came before or after the other wounds?"

"I would think the former. Judging from the blood splatter patterns at the scene that had not been disturbed at the start of the investigation, her heart had stopped before any dismemberment took place. Blood at the scene was splattered in a wide pattern with little drops. Like shaking a wet sponge. If she had still had blood flow, it would have been more concentrated, like liquid from a squirt gun."

The detective nodded to show his understanding as he continued to take notes.

"Detective Farmer," said the doctor in a quieter tone. "This killing was personal."

Farmer's eyebrows raised. He stopped taking notes and caught the doctor in his steely gaze, hanging on to every word. "How so?" he asked just above a whisper.

"This is the most brutal killing I have seen in years. Sam was facing the attacker when he struck."

"He?"

"Detective, the amount of strength used to crush through a skull like that. Hell, it's not like The Walking Dead where they run around poking the zombies through the head easily with a butter knife. He had to strike hard and quick. And the strength required to dismember a body with a blunt object... He didn't cut through the joints. He broke through the bones and managed to force his way through the skin and muscle."

"Brutal!"

"I doubt seriously that a woman would be capable of that power. I can't begin to estimate the number of times the weapon was brought down onto her body. That points to this being personal, but one other finding confirms it."

Detective Farmer was becoming too engrossed in the details to even take notes.

"One other finding, or should I say lack of finding, left no doubt in my mind. Sam's heart. It is nowhere to be found. The killer removed it from her chest by blunt force."

"Blunt force?"

"The killer reached into her chest with his bare hands and ripped her heart out. He must have taken it with him."

The detective swallowed hard. "With him? Why?

"Who knows for sure, but this is an unbelievably sick individual. Perhaps he ate it or kept it as some grotesque trophy."

Chandler swallowed hard. "I can't even imagine."

"No one sane could, detective. You can't replicate the thought process in a mind that sociopathic and sick. It is impossible for the sane mind to comprehend what goes on in that mind. I wish I could have helped more but I couldn't find any additional evidence. All I do know is that it is someone strong and extremely angry. I can say with certainty that this was not some random act of violence by a stranger. Sam knew her killer."

Detective Farmer stood and made his way towards the door. How could he give these details to the chief? The man was already at the breaking point. It had been hard enough to lose his granddaughter but in such a horrific way would be more than anyone could take.

Before the detective could open the door Dr. Kernek stood up behind his desk. "Too bad the poor girl couldn't carry concealed. The outcome could have been very different. A well-made 9mm would have been a game changer."

Detective Farmer nodded in agreement. "I know her grandfather took her to the range often. She could shoot well, but she was only 17."

"I know the law but a well-trained, level-headed 17-year-old girl, I would trust. You know what they say?"

"What's that?"

"Better tried by 12 than carried by 6."

Chandler smiled grimly and nodded before slipping out the door.

A week after the murder, Sam's family and friends joined together at the cemetery to lay the murdered girl to rest. The white casket was slowly lowered into the ground as Ben wiped tears from his eyes and Lily kept her arm around him for support.

School would be back in session on Monday to start the final 6 weeks of the year and the police seemed no closer to catching Sam's killer. All reports from the crime lab pointed to one thing. The crime scene had been poorly preserved in the first hours of the investigation. The fact that the park was so well used by so many made DNA, hair samples, and fingerprints useless. If they could only find the murder weapon perhaps it could yield the evidence they needed. Detective Farmer's investigation was reduced to looking for a freakishly strong, insane man, wearing a size 11 shoe who had an affinity for hearts. Or at least Sam's heart.

Always and Forever

The first real break in the case came a few days later when someone reported a strong, foul odor while walking their dog in the alleyway. The little dog barked and pulled hard against her leash before her owner pulled her away and headed home. The concerned lady contacted the police when she entered her house and reported what she felt to be a dead animal.

Two uniformed officers arrived and walked up the alley. Looking for any sign of a dead cat or raccoon. The faint scent struck the first officer, and he froze in his tracks.

"Damn!" exclaimed the officer as his senses jumped into overdrive.

"What is it, Jack? You looked pretty shook up."

"It's been a few years since I have smelled that. Not since I served in Iraq, but that is death. By God, once you smell it, it haunts your dreams, and you never forget it. That is the smell of death! Rotting human flesh!"

Detective Farmer arrived on the scene as the alley filled with squad cars. Dogs led the investigators to the shed, and it didn't take long to discover the bloody mower blade hanging on the old nail and a curious box stuffed under the back of the shed.

Just before the lunch bell, police descended on the high school. Ben was in science class with Lily and Pete when the police entered the room. Before Mr. Scott could speak two uniformed officers pounced on Pete and pushed him face-first onto the wooden floor.

The entire class sat frozen as if caught in Medusa's gaze. Detective Farmer entered the room as the officers lifted Pete to his feet by his handcuffed arms. He wasted no time with pleasantries and scowled as he raised his voice. "Peter Mathews, you are under arrest for the murder of Samantha Reynolds."

Detective Farmer's stare was cold as he directed the officers holding Pete. "Get that sick bastard out to the cars and read him his rights. I want anything he says written down and admissible. If he resists in any way, and God knows I hope he does, make him pay for it."

No one in the class was more stunned than Ben. Pale and shaking, he jumped to his feet and stared in disbelief at the nightmare unfolding before his eyes. The voice inside his head was screaming louder than a freight train. "NO! This is wrong. It can't be Pete." As much as Ben wanted Sam's killer caught and justly punished, he knew in his heart of hearts that Pete was innocent.

Ben was shaken to his core and Lilly held his hand tight as they walked to her car. Try as she must to remain somber, she couldn't help but flash a brief smile. Ben was now all hers. "I have you, sweetheart," she said as soothing as possible while laughing inside. Poor Ben had no idea how literal and true that statement was. "You can count on me to keep you strong."

"It can't be Pete, Lil. It just can't. Pete couldn't hurt anyone. We were all best friends."

"I'm your best friend now, lover," cooed Lily.

Ben stopped for a moment as he felt anger building inside. "Damn it, Lil! It's not about you. I'm hurting inside and I have no idea which end is up, and which is down. Just a few months ago, the three of us were having lunch and talking about our lives after graduation and now they are gone."

Rage flashed in Lily's eyes, but she was able to quickly recover and turn the flames into tears. "I'm sorry, Ben," she sobbed. "I want to be here for you but I'm new at this. I just don't know how. You must hate me!" Her tears grew in intensity. "I'll just go home. I won't bother you anymore."

Always and Forever

Completely outgunned and manipulated, Ben fell over himself apologizing and crying as well. "I'm sorry, Lil. I just don't know what to do. I'm so sorry. Don't leave me."

Reaching over, Lily pulled Ben close and buried his tear-soaked face into her perfumed shoulder. "It's alright, lover. It's alright. You have me forever," she wickedly smiled. Let me take you home."

John walked into the police station just after 8 pm. The call from Pete's father, Tom, had come as quite a shock and it took the lawyer several minutes to get the frantic man to calm down. The two had been friends since college but John had never heard him so shaken up.

"Slow down, Tom. I can't understand you. You are talking too fast. Okay, that's better. Pete? Little Petie, sure I remember him."

Any hint of a smile the lawyer had from thoughts of forgotten memories disappeared. "Murder? What the hell, Tom? Of course. I'll drop everything."

After the two-hour drive, the lawyer entered the police station confidently and approached the desk sergeant. Holding out his credentials, John spoke calmly, "Sergeant, I'm John Stevens. I have been retained as counsel for Peter Mathews. I need to see my client immediately. Can you please direct me to the juvenile facility?"

The sergeant barely looked up. "He's not there," he grunted. "He's here."

"The boy is seventeen! Why is he here with the adult prisoners?"

"Don't know," he shrugged. "Chief said to keep him here."

"Has he been arraigned?"

"Nope."

"Why not? He is a juvenile with a murder charge."

"Not charged yet. Chief locked him up as a prime suspect so he couldn't interfere while the detective gathered evidence."

"No charges and I would guess no warrant. You can't hold him here. I want to see him now."

The sergeant rose to his feet and shook his index finger in John's face. "Look here! You slimeball lawyers are all alike. This kid killed the Chief's only grandchild. He loved that girl and you come in here making demands. Kiss my ass counsellor! Come back in the morning."

John's face turned red, and his usual mild demeanor stiffened, "Fine, Sergeant. I tried to do this the nice way but apparently you are hell-bent to ruin my night. Why don't I just call Judge Hastings and explain to him that you, yes you, sergeant, are illegally holding a juvenile suspect, without a warrant, in an adult facility and refusing his constitutional right to counsel? Sergeant, that amounts to kidnapping and false imprisonment. Hell, you have just given me more than enough to challenge this whole arrest in court."

The sergeant's smug expression vanished as quickly as his face paled. He began to mutter something, but John abruptly turned and started for the door. "Wait," stammered the sergeant. "I'll take you back to the cell."

John, smiling, simply held up his hand as he continued his march to the door. "Too late!" he shouted back as he breached the door and walked into the street, phone in hand.

At about 9:50, blue lights pierced the night at the entrance to the police station. Moments later, John burst through the doorway followed by two uniformed state troopers and a state juvenile welfare officer.

The sergeant jumped to his feet at the invasion, spilling his coffee on his light blue uniform shirt. He looked on, stunned as John slammed a white paper upon the desk.

"A writ from Judge Hastings. Now, take us to Peter, or these troopers will take you into custody for obstruction."

Other officers in the building could only look on as the sergeant led John and his procession into the holding cells. Peter was lying on the cot in his dimly lit cell, facing the wall with his back to the metal cell door. The boy was lying in a tight fetal position with his knees drawn up tightly against his chest. At the sound of the steel lock clanking open and the cell door creaking, Pete began to whimper and shake violently.

"Pete," called out John in a calm voice. "It's alright now. Your dad sent me to help."

Pete groaned as he tried to turn over to the sound of John's voice but fell off the cot, helplessly to the cold concrete floor. Bright purple bruising, fresh lacerations, and congealed blood, bore testament, even in the dim light, of the vicious beating the boy had endured.

"My God!" exclaimed John in uncontrolled reflex. The stunned lawyer turned towards the sergeant, silently hoping for some answer, however, the jailer only shrugged. "He resisted. Stronger than he looks, he is. The crazy ones always are."

John grabbed the sergeant by the shirt and raised his right fist to strike, but luckily, the two troopers sprang into action and stopped the attack before it could begin.

During the commotion, the welfare officer rushed to Pete's side. "Quick, call an ambulance!" she shouted. "This boy is seriously hurt."

John, after spending the night at the hospital with Pete's father and mother, was looking rather tired and disheveled and was now busy in an early morning meeting with Judge Hastings and the District Attorney.

"Look, I understand that the Chief's granddaughter was killed," said John his stamina and tolerance worn thin. "I get it! But that doesn't entitle the local police force to beat the hell out of a minor. For God's sake, they nearly killed the boy."

"Don't get so dramatic, John," replied the D.A. "I think 'almost killed' is a bit of an exaggeration."

"Oh really, Dave?" replied John, pulling out his notepad. "I just spent the night at the hospital with the family. Let's see here, oh yes. Severe concussion, multiple lacerations on the face and head requiring stitches, A fractured eye socket, and two teeth knocked out. Dramatic? Oh, wait, multiple fractured ribs bilaterally with a punctured collapsed lung on the right. He spent two hours in surgery to repair the lung. No, Dave, I don't think I have been dramatic."

Judge Hastings's bushy gray eyebrows raised slightly. "I'm not a doctor, counsellor but it does sound like almost killed to me."

"They beat the snot out of that boy, your honor, and left him to die in that cell. He wouldn't have made it till morning," said John.

The judge looked sternly at the district attorney. His gray hair and wrinkles bore witness to the many years he had practiced law and sat on the bench. He let out a sigh and shook his head. "Dave, back in the seventies and eighties I would, at times, have cases come before me where the officers perhaps were a little overzealous in their arrest of certain suspects. I remember one particular case involving a forty-seven-year-old man caught in the act of molesting a terrified five-year-old girl. They caught that sick bastard literally in the act. He was in pretty rough shape when he arrived at the station. The pervert did survive the arrest, but I can guarantee he never molested or will molest anyone again."

"Life in prison?" asked Dave.

'No. It seems that there was a serious scuffle during the arrest. His pants were down and 'unexplainably' his balls got caught up on something and were ripped off."

Always and Forever

John and Dave both swallowed hard and unconsciously readjusted the crotch of their pants.

"Point is, a complaint was filed but I couldn't blame the officers. They were family men with children of their own. That was a different time and severe circumstances. I haven't seen this kind of mistreatment in decades. This boy wasn't caught in the act of anything and is a boy! I can't sit by and let grown men beat a kid nearly to death because they 'think' he might have done something. That makes them more like that 5-year-old's molester than her saviors."

"I think I understand, your honor," said the district attorney somberly. "My office and the department's internal affairs will investigate it."

"Dave, you need this investigated by an external agency. Think of the optics. The people here would never trust the department to investigate its own. I don't want the folks here scared to call the police because they might get someone beaten. I don't care how the department or the chief feels about this. I want any, and I mean any, officer involved or complicit in this beating prosecuted. Did you understand that, Counsellor? Prosecuted."

Dave looked stunned for a moment but then nodded in agreement. "Yes, sir."

John didn't envy Dave for the position the police had put him in but continued to push ahead while he had the advantage. "Any statement my client made while in custody is inadmissible. Never happened. I don't think I would have any trouble convincing any jury that it was coerced."

"Agreed," said the judge. "So, Dave, are you pursuing an inditement?"

"Yes, your honor. It's scheduled for the grand jury the afternoon."

"What do you have to make your case?" asked John.

"We have the murder weapon from the boy's shed, footprints in the blood at the scene matching the boy's size, and we found Sam's heart buried beneath the back of the boy's shed."

"Any prints on the weapon?" asked John.

"We are evaluating it now," replied Dave. "It was very rusty and bloody. We sent it to the state crime lab for testing. Our lab here isn't equipped to handle it. We also sent the heart and the container it was found in for testing."

"And you will let me know when the results come in?" asked John.

"Of course. It is part of discovery. I don't expect results for a week or so, but I'll have the lab forward the results to your office at the same time they send mine."

"All right then gentlemen," said the tired judge. "It sounds like we are done here, and I need to get some breakfast before I start my normal workday. The boy will be guarded at the hospital by the state police. Due to circumstances, I am granting release to his parents. I know Mr. Mathews and know he will follow the court's directions. Besides it sounds like the boy won't be leaving the hospital any time soon."

"Why the guard then?" asked John.

"To keep anything else from happening. The local police aren't the only folks here who would like to see the boy dead. I'm ordering protective custody for the boy pending trial."

"Thank you, your honor," said John with a nod.

"In the meantime, Dave, I would strongly suggest that you meet with the chief as soon as possible. Tell him to get his department under control. I want to see suspensions and charges filed. I want to see it on tonight's news and read about it in tomorrow's paper. I want the message sent that anyone who harms that boy before trial will suffer consequences. I want a fair trial and not a lynch mob."

"Understood," agreed the district attorney as he rose to his feet. "I agree, we want justice."

Word of Pete's arrest spread through the town like a raging tornado quickly followed by news of the beating and hospitalization. Ben, still sure of Pete's innocence, asked Lily to take him to the hospital across town to see him and try to understand what had happened.

"This is such a horrible mistake," sighed Ben as they drove. "No way in hell Pete could do such a thing."

Lily kept looking ahead. "I'm sure you're right, lover. Of course, I don't know him as well as you do but I'm sure you're right."

The normally quiet community hospital was buzzing with activity. About 2 dozen protesters were carrying signs and chanting outside the main entrance. Many others, curious of the spectacle, were quietly standing to the side. The main entrance was locked up tight with a sign directing all patients and staff to the guarded Emergency Room entrance for screening and entrance to the hospital.

Ben and Lily timidly approached the E.R. and were met by a state trooper standing guard. "Do you have an emergency or an appointment?"

"Neither," replied Ben quietly. "I'm here to talk to Peter Mathews. I'm his best friend."

The trooper looked sympathetic. "Sorry, the hospital is on lockdown for the next day or so. Only patients allowed."

"Oh, sorry. I didn't know" said Ben dropping his head in disappointment. "I know he didn't do anything wrong, and I just wanted to talk to him and let him know I have faith in him."

"I understand friendship, I do. But I can't let anyone in. Besides, your buddy had a pretty rough time of it. My partners upstairs say it could be a day or so before he will be awake enough to talk anyway. Tell you what. Write what you want to tell him on this notepad and when I take my turn upstairs, I'll give it to his family to give him when he wakes up."

"Thank you, sir," said Ben smiling as he eagerly took the notepad and began writing.

"You seem like a good kid and a good friend, but if I were you, I really wouldn't walk around announcing that friendship. Some of these folks out here are ready to string him up, guilty or not. If they can't get to him, they might find you to be the next best thing."

Ben finished the note and handed it to the trooper. "Thank you, sir. I will be careful."

Lily took Ben's hand and led him back over to her car. "Sorry, lover. Maybe you can see him soon."

Ben forced a weak smile and cried on Lily's shoulder.

The school became constant whispering about the murder and Pete's arrest. Wild rumors and theories swirled through the hallways and classes about cannibalism and satanic rituals conducted in the park under cover of darkness. Some were even sure they had heard that Sam had been pregnant by Pete, and he had killed her to rectify the situation. Ben did his best to ignore the whispers and Lily did her best to never let Ben out of her sight.

After a week of torment, whispers quieted, and students were finally getting back to their studies. Ben got word that Pete was awake and out of danger. Life was becoming tolerable.

Always and Forever

Tuesday's fourth-period A&P class started with the usual last-minute scurrying of students to take their seats. Ben sat at his desk and stared at his angel sitting at the window. Taking comfort as the angel stared back.

Mr. Scott walked down the aisle collecting homework assignments and paused at Ben's desk. The teacher's frustration finally showed as Ben, again, had forgotten or ignored the day's assignment.

"Ben, not again. I know things have been tough for you, but you have to focus and get these assignments in. Your grades can't take much more of this behavior."

A shout suddenly came from the other side of the room and Mr. Scott turned just in time to catch a flying textbook with his nose and mouth. Lily stood at the window screaming at the science teacher as he fell to one knee from the blow. "You leave Ben alone, you jealous bastard! You just can't stand that he's smarter than you!"

The boys in the class jumped up and restrained Lil as she prepared to hurl another tome at the stunned teacher. Ben just sat in disbelief as they pulled Lily, still screaming, into the hallway. As the door closed behind them, Mr. Scott looked up at Ben, blood pouring from his broken nose and split lip onto the white tile floor.

That evening Ben sat in the shadows outside the police station when Mrs. Greene escorted her daughter out the door to their waiting car. He considered going up to the door, but he had no idea what he would say to Lily or her mother. After watching them drive away, he turned and walked slowly home.

He had only been home for a half hour when his cell phone rang. "Ben, it's me."

"Are you alright?"

"I'm fine. I just couldn't let that little prick talk to you like that. He'd be happy to have half your brain."

"Come on, baby, don't talk like that. I'm worried about you. Have they told you what they plan to do?"

"The cops are going to charge me with assault, but I'll probably just have to pick up trash or something on the weekend. I can't go back to school until Monday. That's when they'll have a hearing to see if I can come back at all."

"I'll do whatever I can to help. Just let me know. Maybe you could plead temporary insanity. You know, some hormonal thing."

"Don't worry about it. If they kick me out, then we can just have more time together."

"If they kick you out, I'll still have to go."

"Oh, come on now, lover. You'd skip school to be with me, wouldn't you?

Ben thought hard for a moment but wasn't sure he was ready to flush away any plans for college and a career. "You worry too much, Lil. I'm sure once you've apologized to Mr. Scott and things have died down over the weekend, they'll let you back in."

"I am not going to apologize to him," fumed Lily. "He was wrong to…"

"Baby, you have to tell him you're sorry. There's no hope of them letting you come back if you don't. Come on, angel, do it for me."

Lily's voice softened, "If you want me to, then I'll do it. I'll tell him I'm sorry and he'll believe me, but I won't mean it."

"That's my girl."

"I love being your girl. Can I see you tonight?"

Always and Forever

"It's getting kinda late and I think we've had enough excitement for today. I'll come by right after school tomorrow, okay?"

"You have to promise. I'll just die if I can't see you tomorrow."

Ben laughed. "Of course, I promise."

As Ben walked down the hallway Wednesday everyone wanted to know about Lily and what they referred to as the incident. Ben was just glad that the talk of the school had now shifted from Pete. He realized that this was the first time since he and Lily had gotten together that he was able to walk the school hall alone. He did miss her but enjoyed the time to speak to his friends and catch his breath.

With the final bell, Ben gathered his books and set out for Lily's house. The girl was waiting on her front step as Ben turned the corner.

Lil jumped up as he approached and threw her arms around him as if they had been apart for months. "I've missed you so much. I had no idea what to do all day without you beside me. I've been sitting here thinking about what our kids will be like."

"Our kids!?" said Ben, pulling her arms down. "Why did you wig out on Mr. Scott like that?"

"I don't know. I guess I just lost my temper at the way he was picking on you."

"Lil, he just fussed a little because I forgot my homework again. Baby, you broke his nose. He didn't come to school today and might not be back tomorrow. I know everything has been insane with what's happened to Sam and the mistake with Pete. I have been a basket case myself and I know I have put a lot of stress on you. I will talk to the principal tomorrow and see if it will help. I feel like it's all my fault."

Lily sat next to Ben on the step. "It's not your fault, it's mine, but still again you rush to my aid like the hero you are. I don't know what happened in my head. I just love you so much, and if he hadn't stopped talking to you like that, I think I would have killed him."

Ben's blood ran cold at the confession. "Stop being so dramatic. If anyone heard you, they might think you were serious."

His angel turned and looked coldly into his eyes. "I do mean it. If anyone hurt you or tried to take you from me, I would kill them."

Ben was speechless, and the girl continued. "You're part of me now. I can't let anyone separate us. If you left me, I'd kill myself."

"You can't mean that," said Ben as all the color drained from his face.

Lily laughed and kissed the startled boy's pale cheek. "Of course I mean it. But I'd have to kill you first, silly boy. Not that it would ever come to that; I know you'll never leave me."

Ben continued looking into Lily's eyes, hoping for the slightest hint of teasing, but her eyes stared unflinchingly until she smiled softly and kissed his cheek. She whispered in his ear, "We belong to each other, forever."

Later that afternoon a stunned Ben walked home slowly wondering what he had done. Looking up, he saw that he was passing Greg's house. He hadn't talked to Greg since Lily had come into his life, but the blue Firebird was parked in the drive, so he wandered up to the door and knocked on it.

Greg opened the door with a smile and reached his hand out to Ben. "Hey, buddy. I'm surprised to see you. Shouldn't you and Lily be making out somewhere?"

Ben shook his head. "It's all wrong. I wanted her so badly but it's just all wrong."

Greg's smile vanished. "What happened?"

"I have a homicidal psychopath proclaiming her undying love to me and naming our children, that's what happened. You heard what she did to Mr. Scott, and now she claims she'll kill me and then herself if she thinks I'm leaving her."

"She can't mean it. Girls say all kinds of things to keep you from breaking their hearts."

"Oh, she means it alright. She's also sworn to kill any girl that tries to take me away from her. I think that's why she attacked Scott. She must think his griping about my homework will scare me into studying more and take time away from her."

Just then Ben's cell phone rang. Looking at the caller ID, he rolled his eyes and announced, "It's her."

"Well, you'd better answer it," responded Greg.

Ben hit the speaker button. "Hello."

"Ben. Is everything okay?!" Lily asked, the concern strong in her voice.

"Sure. Why wouldn't it be?"

"You said you were going home but I just called your house and your mother said she hasn't seen you yet."

"No, I'm still on my way."

"Don't lie to me!" snapped Lily. "It takes twenty minutes to walk from my house to yours and it's been twenty-eight minutes since you left here."

"You're timing me?" said Ben, astonished by what he had just heard.

"I want to make sure you're safe, that's all."

"I just stopped to talk with Greg for a moment."

"Is he alone?"

"What do you mean?" asked Ben.

"Are there girls there? Why won't you tell me instead of avoiding the question? You didn't say you were going to Greg's. You said you were going home."

Ben became angry but decided to tread lightly. "No, lover, there are no girls here. It's just me and Greg talking outside his house. I was just telling him the names you picked out for our kids. I was just leaving to head home. Sorry for worrying you."

Lily's tone changed as if Ben had flipped a switch. "You are so sweet. I'm sorry for being fussy. Still love me?"

"Of course I do. I'll call you when I get home."

"Call me from the house phone so I'll know it's you by the caller ID."

Ben exhaled. "Sure, baby. I'll call you soon."

Snapping the phone closed Ben looked at the stunned Greg. "See what I mean? She even insists I call her on the house phone to prove I'm not lying about being home."

"Sorry man, I don't know what to say. But if I were you, which I'm glad I'm not, I'd hurry home and give her a call before she grabs a meat cleaver and comes looking for your ass. Maybe she has just temporarily snapped with all the drama at school."

Ben rushed home and walked in through the door just as the phone began to ring.

"Hello?"

"Ben! Why didn't you call me like you promised? I was worried."

"Lily," Ben replied through clenched teeth, "I just walked through the door. I practically ran home from Greg's. I'm here now, so you can stop worrying."

"Can you talk for a while? I've been thinking more about our future."

"We'll talk tomorrow. I have to get some homework done so we can have a future."

"You're not going anywhere, are you?"

"No, I'll be right here at the house. I'll call you later."

"Love me?"

"Yes, but I must go. Bye"

Ben was in a panic as he hung up the kitchen phone and went down the hall to his room. As he walked into the bedroom, he was shocked, but pleased, to see Lucifer sitting by his window.

"What have you done to me!?" cursed Ben in a muffled voice so as not to alarm his parents in the living room.

"Gave you the desires of your heart, just like I promised. Why? Isn't everything going well?"

"You know damn well things aren't going well. You planned all this from the start."

The Devil laughed. "Now why wouldn't I want you to be happy?"

"I want out! Make her stop loving me. I don't care what it costs."

"Sorry, Ben. I can't break the contract and you have nothing left to buy me out. I already have your soul and that's all I deal in."

"Keep my soul. I don't care. I just want her out of my life."

"For a bright lad, you don't seem to listen very well. I fully intend to keep your soul and have you keep the girl. The contract was simple - you got what you wanted, and I got what I wanted. Our deal is done."

Ben glared at the Devil as he looked out the window stroking his beard.

"Wait," said Satan, as if he just had an epiphany. "I know what we can do."

"What?" Ben asked desperately.

"I'll sell you back your contract in exchange for two clean souls. It will be a kind of one-for-two sale," said the Devil with a laugh.

"What do you mean, clean souls?"

"You know. Ones I don't already have influence over. Folks like you used to be. That is before you stole those tests. You see, unless someone strays from the straight and narrow, they're protected. I can't even make my sales pitch."

Ben looked doubtful and stammered, "You mean an innocent person. You're holding my soul ransom to make me do your bidding. There must be another way."

Lucifer just looked back out the window. "No, I can't think of any. And the ransom, as you so eloquently put it, is small. Souls are my only currency. All you have to do is open the door for me, and I'll do the rest. If two people sign up then you're off the hook, and I'll see to it that Lily moves on."

"No," said Ben shaking his head. "I won't do it. I won't let you ruin anyone else's life. I can help her through this and then we can be happy like we first were."

"Suit yourself," chuckled Satan. "Just remember I'm not like your own personal genie that you can summon at will. I'm very busy these days but I may check on you later. You just never know."

Ben turned to a sound from the living room but when he turned back Satan had vanished.

Laying there that night in the dark, Ben tossed and turned, unable to quiet his racing mind. How could things have gotten so out of hand? How could he break his contract without hurting anyone in the process? Tears came and Ben finally fell asleep on his wet pillow.

Always and Forever

The Grand Jury, as expected, returned a capital murder indictment for Pete, and about ten days later, John received a fax from the crime lab with all the forensic test results. Within the hour, Dave's phone at the DA's office began to ring.

"Dave? It's John. Did you review the test results on the Peter Mathews case? Good! Can we meet tomorrow at 1? 1:30 then. No problem I'll be there."

John walked into the District Attorney's office at 1:15 and checked in. It was only a minute or so before Dave's paralegal called John back to the office.

John walked into the comfortable office and nodded to Dave, sitting at the desk behind several files. The air seemed thick and tense as John sat back in a plush leather chair and waited for Dave to speak. After what seemed like a very long minute John couldn't wait any longer and cut to the chase. "So, are you going to push ahead with this case?"

"I don't know," replied Dave with exasperation.

"The mower blade had only prints from Peter's father and only Samatha's blood and DNA. You have bloody size 11 shoeprints but not the shoes that made them. The heart, and the box it was found in, had no fingerprints and no DNA other than Samantha's. The park was full of hair, fiber, and prints from half the town. Please, Dave! Prosecute this case so I can get a not guilty verdict for my client."

"I just know this kid did it, John. I just can't prove it."

"Come on, counsellor. You 'know' he is guilty, or you 'want' him to be guilty? Do you honestly think this kid could be such a criminal mastermind to do all he did and leave not a shred of evidence and then be so stupid to take the murder weapon and heart home to hide them in his backyard?"

Dave hung his head. "Fine, yes, I want him to be guilty! That would mean that the police didn't beat the living hell out of an innocent teenager, and we don't still have a deranged psychopath wandering loose."

"I get it, Dave. I do, but I've known this kid's father since college. That boy didn't do it."

"I'll release a statement this afternoon stating that the DA office is not pursuing charges at this time."

"At this time? You must be kidding me! You might as well hang a sign on the boy's back saying, 'Shoot me'."

"I'm not ready to exonerate the boy in the press. What if something comes up?"

"Then charge him. It's not like double jeopardy. It's just the press. You owe him and his family that much."

Later that early afternoon, the DA called the press conference, as promised, and Dave approached the microphones. "I have a quick statement and will not be taking any questions. After an exhaustive review of the evidence gathered in the Samantha Reynolds' murder case, the district attorney's office has found nothing to implicate Peter Mathews in the homicide. All charges have been dismissed and Peter Mathews is not a person of interest. The police department is re-opening the investigation in hopes of finding the perpetrator or perpetrators responsible for this horrific crime."

Ben's heart jumped for joy at the announcement made over the school loudspeaker. Lily apologized to Mr. Scott and agreed to 20 hours of community service and 10 days suspension. The girl's behavior had mellowed, and Ben was now hopeful that life might return to some semblance of order.

That evening, Ben's phone rang, and a familiar voice completed Ben's joy.

Always and Forever

"Hey, buddy. I got your note in the hospital. It helped to know you believed me."

"Pete! Of course, I believed you. When are you coming home?"

"Tomorrow afternoon. I'm still plenty sore but everything is healing up pretty well."

"Can I come over after school?"

"I am counting on it."

"I'll come straight over then. Get some rest, man. Damn! I am so happy they cleared you."

"Not more than me. See you tomorrow."

Ben made his nightly phone call to Lily and excitedly told her about Pete. "I know you are not allowed to be at the school for a few more days, but will you be done with community service in time to pick me up after the bell? I want you with me to go see Pete."

"Sure, lover," said Lily with a smile in her voice and a frown on her face. "I'll pick you up at the gas station."

"Thanks, baby. I am so glad everything will get back to normal. You will be back at school next week and we can have more time together."

Now Lily was smiling. Ben was learning how to keep his angel happy and more stable. Perhaps, now that pressure was decreasing, she would stop saying such alarming things.

Ben practically ran to the gas station after the final bell to find Lily waiting. It worried Lily to see Ben happier than he had been in quite a while. As they drove towards Pete's, Lily voiced her concerns, "Lover, you're not going to need me now that Pete's back."

"Don't be silly, sweetheart. I will need you more than ever. Sure, Pete's a friend but, I love you."

Lily tried to smile but didn't seem fully convinced. Ben reached over, took her hand, and squeezed it.

"More than ever?" she asked.

"More than ever!"

Lily was smiling as she and Ben walked into Pete's living room and found him sitting in a recliner.

"Ben! Lily! This is great. I would get up, but things are still a little tender."

Ben was horrified to see the residual swelling and bruising on Pete's face. Try as he could to hide it, Pete knew his buddy. "Don't let my shiner surprise you. It looks so much better now. Besides, you should see the other guy."

Ben sat on the brown, leather sofa across from Pete with Lily practically in his lap.

"Damn, Pete. That had to hurt!"

"More than you know… but pills sure do help. My motto now is 'better life through pharmaceuticals'. One of the punches I took broke my cheekbone and orbit for my eye. The vision in the eye hasn't fully returned but they are hopeful. With that, and the broken ribs, I think it is safe to say I won't be in school tomorrow."

Ben shook his head. "I'm sorry, man. I didn't know."

"I know that. But even if you did, it wouldn't have mattered. I know they wouldn't let you in to see me. The nice thing is that 5 officers are now facing felony charges and John, my lawyer, says I won't have to worry about my college or future now."

"Well, that's good, but I still don't think it was worth it."

"I have to agree," said Pete, with a groan. "But it is what it is."

Always and Forever

"Dad said that since I won't be going back to school this year, he is taking a temporary position at a branch in Denver, and we will be there for about a year. He is also worried that since they haven't caught the real killer yet, some of the folks around here might still blame me and I won't be safe."

"Denver? That's close to a thousand miles away!"

Lily had been silent this whole time but now spoke up. "I think your father is smart, Pete. Best you take time to heal and the police time to catch the real killer. We will miss you, but a year won't be so long. I'll take care of Ben while you're gone."

Pete smiled but Ben could see in his eyes that his friend was not all that happy about leaving town. Even though Ben knew Lily was supporting the decision for her reasons, deep down he knew it would be best for Pete's safety and recuperation.

It only took about an hour for Pete to show signs of exhaustion. Ben and Lily made their way out and decided to spend their time together at the pizza parlor.

About 9 o'clock, Lily dropped off Ben at his home to study. Ben wasted no time racing to his room and calling Pete. "Hey buddy, did you get any rest?"

"I slept some, but I think I will be going to bed for the night soon. I was so glad you came over. You have no idea how it feels to have everyone think you're a monster. You and my family were the only ones that stood by me. That means a lot."

"I knew you couldn't have done it."

"Thanks. By the way, it looks like you and Lily are getting pretty serious."

"She is. You heard about her going all nuts at school. I've been trying to keep her calm, but she has a real jealousy issue. I know why you have to leave but I wish you didn't. I could use a buffer. Sometimes I feel so trapped."

"Break up with her. You can't live like that."

"I wish I could," sighed Ben. "It's a lot more complicated than you know."

"Did you get her pregnant?" asked Pete, sounding shocked.

"No! We haven't even done that. I know she would be game for it, but I have always thought I should wait. I don't think we could have a future, but I have to figure a way out without her completely losing it."

"You know, a lot of guys would take your place in an instant. She is 'model' gorgeous."

"Yeah, but I've learned that looks aren't everything. Crap! I've got to go. She's calling."

The next day after school, Ben and Lily stopped by again to see Pete. The visit was shortened when Pete announced that he needed rest because his father was driving him out to Denver the next morning. Ben felt his heart sink with the news, but Lily was right there to reassure him that he would always have her.

With Pete gone, Lily seemed to relax her grip on Ben a little and started back at school at the end of her suspension. Many of the students were uncertain about Ben's girlfriend and avoided her in the hallways. Any girl standing near Ben when Lily approached fled the area and Ben realized that other students were now afraid to talk to him.

That night, sitting in Lily's car, Ben brought up the subject of college.

"I don't like the idea of you going to college, lover. High school keeps us apart enough. Even when we get married before you start school, like we planned, I wouldn't get to see you enough."

Always and Forever

"Married? When did we decide to get married?"

Lily looked alarmed. "You don't want to marry me? You want me gone?"

"I didn't say that."

"I'm not stupid!" shouted Lily. "You found someone else and are leaving to go to college with her. You prick! I will not let someone else have what's mine!"

"Lily," said Ben, starting to shake. "I never said any of that. I swear, there is no one else. I just didn't remember making wedding plans."

Lily's breathing started to slow. "No one else?"

Ben raised his right hand, "No one! I swear, no one."

"So, we are getting married? You still love me?"

"Baby, of course, I still love you."

Lily smiled and grabbed Ben's hand. "I am so sorry I got upset. I just can't bear the thought of being apart from you."

Ben's defenses began to relax. "You did worry me a little. I wasn't sure what you were going to do."

"Well, lover," responded Lily calmly. "I can't let anyone else have what's mine. I thought for a moment that I would have to kill you and then myself."

Ben's blood ran cold, but he managed to hold his feelings together for the next hour before going inside.

Ben wasn't surprised to see the Devil once again standing in his room, looking out the window. The boy was angry but knew he had to keep his voice down. "This is not what I bargained for! You cheat."

Satan continued to look out the window. "It is exactly what you bargained for, boy. Exactly! How dare you call me a cheat."

"I didn't ask for an insane girlfriend. If she even 'thinks' I'm leaving her, she says she will kill me, and I believe her."

"Oh, I would believe her if I were you. And actually, you did ask for an insane girlfriend," chuckled Satan. She's been insane all along. You just didn't bother to know her before you made up your mind. Look, I gave you a way out. I still have those names…if you want them. All you have to do is ask."

"You would like that, wouldn't you? That's what Greg did. He wanted out of a deal, so he gave you me."

"Actually, you gave me you, but yes, Greg did want out of a deal he had made."

"I can't do that to someone. I just can't. Hey, wait!" said Ben with a sudden idea. "You already own my soul, so it doesn't matter to me. I could just kill Lily before she ends up killing me. Then I won't have to hurt innocent people. I just have to think of a way to not get caught; an accident maybe."

"Hmmm," replied the Devil. "You may be on to something. You realize that I'll still have your contract. But would you be willing to kill the love of your life?"

"I don't love her!"

"But you said you did. You said you wanted her by you, forever."

Ben exhaled and sat on the edge of the bed. A few tears started down his cheek. "I thought I did but I realize now that you are right, I didn't even know her. She's just so beautiful."

"Oh," smirked the Devil. "You must have gotten love confused with lust. Don't feel bad; I deal with people who make that mistake all the time."

"I'll bet you do. You must deal with killing a lot too. Any ideas on how I might go about it?"

"I think your accident idea might bear fruit, but I usually leave these details alone, for people to decide. I wouldn't want to be accused of interfering. I'll check back with you later to see how things are going. You might change your mind and accept my ransom offer. Bye now."

Before Ben could respond the Devil disappeared leaving only a slight scent of sulfur hanging in the air.

The rest of the evening, Ben planned his next move. First, he would have a serious talk with Lil and see if he could soften her violent feelings, but he knew it was probably pointless. If she did come around to reason, he would suspend his plan to see where the relationship might go. But if his fears were justified, then he would act Friday night.

His resolve was strengthened when Lil called later that night. Ben was as calm and reassuring as possible, and Lil was thrilled when he offered to meet her after class to discuss their future together.

His angel cried out with glee to see her beau walking up to her home carrying a single red rose. He greeted her with a warm kiss and the two walked over to the next street and sat under a large tree in the park.

The young man tried flattery. He tried reasoning. After that, he tried the two combined, but just as he felt he was making headway Lil would say something to make the hair on the back of his neck stand up. He sighed with the realization that the poor girl was as mentally disturbed and dangerous as she was beautiful. It felt odd to be plotting her murder as he sat mesmerized by her angelic face and captivating eyes. Never had he considered murder to be justified but now, faced with his self-preservation, it seemed the only solution. He'd humor her until tomorrow night and then end it.

"Tomorrow's Friday," announced Ben as he gave his angel a squeeze. "Let's go out. We can stay out late, and after this week, I think we could both use some time to unwind. I have a friend who works the Quick Stop, and he'll let me buy wine coolers without an ID."

"Just us, out relaxing? No friends or problems to get in the way?" asked Lil

"None whatsoever," promised Ben with a smile.

Lily threw her arms around Ben and gave him a quick kiss. "I love it. Can we get strawberry?"

"Sure, whatever you like. We can take your car up to the point, sit out on a blanket, and watch the stars. It'll be great."

"You'll just get me drunk and have your way with me," giggled Lil.

"You never can tell," said Ben with a sly smile. "You never can tell."

Ben whistled as he walked home. Wine coolers and Lily's dislike of seatbelts would seal her fate and he would be free to move ahead with his life. It all seemed too easy, but he still hated thinking of the detour his life had taken and where his ultimate destination would be. Ben sadly realized that since Lucifer had entered his life, he now was much more comfortable with things that would have repulsed him only a few months before. He shook his head and looked up to the sky. He simply wouldn't dwell on it and just live his life one day at a time.

That Friday night, lying on the soft blanket, Ben looked into the depths of the heavens and thought of how the night sky reminded him of a black velvet tapestry studded with bright diamonds. The wine coolers had greatly softened Lily's mood and she became very affectionate. As she emptied a bottle, Ben was quick to supply her with another. Lily lay against him on the blanket and poured out her heart as she kissed him passionately and pulled at the buttons on his shirt. She was even more beautiful by the moonlight and Ben began to wonder if he was being a little hasty with his plans to end the girl's life. If he could just find a way to keep her isolated and inebriated, life would be good.

As the empty bottles piled up, Lily's speech became more slurred, "I'm so glad that Pete's gone and I killed the bitch, Sam. They were trying to take you away from me."

"You killed Sam?" exclaimed Ben.

"Oops, I shouldn't tell secrets," giggled Lily. "Now, you'll hate me, and I'll have to kill you too."

Ben used all the strength he had to regain control. He was almost free and soon she would be gone. "No, baby, I'm not mad. I know she was trying to break us apart. You were just protecting me."

"She was! She wanted you for herself. I'm just happy Pete moved away," she laughed again. "There for minute I thought he was going to have to commit suicide."

"It's alright now. We have each other. Here, only three wine coolers left."

Ben had managed to limit his consumption to two bottles and pushed more to Lily. In about 45 minutes she passed out.

Determined, but still feeling a little dizzy, he carried Lily's limp form to the passenger's side of the car. He placed her in carefully and closed the door. Ben walked around the car a few times to think things through one last time before bravely getting behind the steering wheel and turning the ignition.

He started down the dark road with Lily, as beautiful as ever, sleeping against the passenger door. Soon the yellow warning sign for the iron, one-lane bridge came into view, and Ben took a deep breath and accelerated hard. He glanced one last time at Lily as he reached over with his right hand, brought his seatbelt tab over, and clicked it into the buckle.

The car sped along at about seventy when the iron bridge abutment was illuminated by the bright headlights. Ben gripped the steering wheel tight and then heard Lily's soft voice, "Ben, your seat belt buckle is broken."

The impact was tremendous and could be heard echoing through the hills, as charging steel and plastic gave way to unyielding rusty iron. To Ben, it was as if everything happened in slow motion. Glass from the buckling windshield exploded into the car, spraying his face and chest. The seatbelt tab pulled easily free from the broken buckle as his momentum carried his body forward, slamming violently into the steering wheel and dash. His legs became twisted and caught in the pedals, exerting great pressure on the bones until they loudly snapped, allowing him to continue forward. His ears filled with the sounds of twisting metal and screams of agony. Whether the screams were his or Lily's he didn't know.

Ben fell back into the seat as his forward momentum ceased and he was suddenly blinded by bright light as flames shot hungrily into the car from the damaged engine. As Ben faded into blackness, he felt two hands grab his shoulders and pull.

Ben opened his eyes to find himself sitting in a plush leather chair. Lining the walls and stretching to the ceiling were massive bookcases filled with old books and scrolls. The room was illuminated by a sole ornate fireplace directly in front of the chair. As he looked around and prepared to stand a dark figure stepped out from the shadows.

"Greetings, Ben," said Lucifer.

"Where am I?" asked the startled boy.

"Why, you're in my study," replied Lucifer calmly. "It seems your little plot has backfired."

"I'm dead?"

Always and Forever

"I guess I can't pull the wool over your eyes. Welcome to your new home. Well, I guess this isn't your new home. This is mine. Yours isn't quite as nice, but I'll take you to it now."

Ben's head hung low as he followed the Devil from the mansion and into a barren dark landscape. The air was hot and smelled of sulfur. It hit Ben's skin like a blast furnace and burned his nose and throat. As they drew further from the mansion the discomfort became pain.

"Where do I stay? Where's my new home?" asked Ben, gasping for air, and gritting his teeth.

"Straight ahead," said Lucifer, pointing to the horizon.

Looking hard into the darkness, Ben could just make out black flames licking skyward. "Out there?"

"That's it," replied the Devil. "Just keep moving forward towards the screams. I'm sure someone there will show you around." Lucifer turned to head back toward the mansion. Ben grabbed his hand and fell to his knees.

"No! This can't be happening," begged Ben. "Please, I need another chance!"

"Everyone always wants another chance!" shouted Lucifer. "You didn't want to take the offer I made earlier! You thought you were smart and wanted to manage things on your own!"

The boy cried and fell to the Devil's feet begging for mercy. Finally, Lucifer kicked the boy's face, "Shut up! I can't stand your spineless sniveling. I'll offer you the same deal I made you before. Take it or leave it."

"You mean two souls for mine?"

"You help me with two souls, and I'll tear up your contract. Do we have a deal?"

"How will I find two souls that are innocent?"

"Well, I will happily admit that they are much harder to find than they were a few years ago. I've had great success employing movies and the internet to gain control, but I can still guide you to a few that will do nicely."

"Then give me a chance," cried Ben. "I won't let you down."

"So be it."

Ben was enveloped in darkness, but the pain subsided. The world around him was as comforting and secure as a warm blanket except for a steady, incessant beeping. Time crept by slowly, days, weeks, or months, Ben couldn't tell. Finally, the beeping grew louder until Ben could stand it no more and his eyes burst open to see the white ceiling of a hospital room.

He reached up to find a thick tube coming from his mouth and multiple tubes attached to each arm. Rolling his head to the right, towards the source of the beeping, he saw a heart monitor showing eighty beats per minute and a blood pressure of 140 over 70. He was alive.

Over the next day or so Ben found out that although he was alive, he had suffered greatly in the accident. He had broken his back when he slammed into the steering wheel and was now paralyzed from the abdomen down, and his arms were now considerably weaker. However, on the third day after waking up, his greatest horror was realized. His parents had just left for the day, and Ben was drifting off to sleep when he was jolted back to consciousness by her voice. "Hi, lover! I thought I lost you."

He snapped his head to the doorway to see Lily limping into the room on crutches. It was Lily, but his angel also suffered from the accident. Aside from her broken leg, Ben was horrified to see her face. Multiple red scars on her forehead bore silent witness to her impact with the windshield, and large thick patches of pink skin covered the right side of her face and neck. It distorted the side of her mouth and made her right eye constantly partially closed. Most of her golden hair was gone with only patches showing any promise of returning.

She sat next to him and carefully took his hand into hers. The once soft delicate skin of her hands was now rough and unyielding. "I was thrown free of the crash when we hit the bridge, but as I was pulling you free from the steering wheel the car caught fire. I guess I got a little singed, but we made it."

"A little singed?" thought Ben. To him, it looked as if she had stopped a grenade blast with her face.

"Don't worry, Ben. Your paralysis makes no difference to me. I love you and I'll look after you forever. I told your parents that we're getting married after you leave the hospital and I'll nurse you back to health."

"Please, Lil. I need to sleep. Let's talk about this tomorrow."

"Alright, lover. I'll see you tomorrow. I love you," she whispered as she brought her scarred lip to his cheek.

That night, as Ben lay quietly, his nose detected a faint smell of sulfur. Turning toward the window he spotted Lucifer sitting in the visitor's chair.

"A young, pretty, student nurse named Jennifer will be on duty taking care of you tonight. Talk her into sneaking a six-pack of beer into the hospital to share with you. You do that and I'll take care of the rest."

"I don't know if I can."

"Because you don't know how or don't want to?"

"Both really," said Ben, feeling very guilty about being responsible for corrupting someone innocent.

"Fine, you little lying prick. Spend the rest of your life with Scarface and come back to Hell when you die."

"But I'm the reason she looks like that. I hurt her."

"Sure, you did… but remember she was going to end up killing you. It was self-defense. She deserved it."

Ben thought hard. "I guess you're right, but to corrupt someone…"

"Look, did Greg hold a gun to your head and demand the tests? No, he did not! He simply put an opportunity in front of you. It was your choice to do as he asked. And your choice to sign my contract for that matter. It was always your choice. All you ever had to do was say no."

"Okay, fine, but how do I do it?"

"Now we're talking, boy. Once you get Jennifer's attention and trust, simply lay on the peer pressure."

"Peer pressure?"

"Sure, you know… It's okay, everybody does it. Don't worry, nobody's getting hurt. It's only wrong if we get caught and we'll be careful. Peer pressure has always been my greatest tool. Who do you think invented it?" said Satan with a hearty laugh.

Ben nodded and smiled weakly.

"Besides," continued Lucifer. "If you're lucky enough to pull this off, I already have a second person in mind. There's a good chance you can have your contract back by the end of the month.

Lucifer vanished, and within the hour Jenn showed up as promised. Ben did as the Devil instructed and was able to get her to sit and talk with him into the night. Finally, using sympathy and half-truths, he was able to get the young girl to agree to sneak in the beer.

When she showed up the next night Ben begged Jennifer to sit and have one too so that he wouldn't be drinking alone. It couldn't hurt to have just one, and Ben had gum in his nightstand to hide the beer smell on her breath. She smiled and they toasted their new friendship behind the hospital curtain.

The next week Ben was released from the hospital, and as arranged and in the interest of his safety, he and Lily were married by the local judge. Within days Ben crossed paths with a young lad Lucifer was interested in. Ben put his newly honed skills to work and was successful in opening a door for the Devil to make his sales pitch.

A few days later, Ben was wheeled into the apartment by his new bride to find Lucifer waiting for him. Lily was alarmed but quieted down when Ben introduced him as his uncle from out east. As Lil was busy pouring coffee in the kitchen, Lucifer smiled and presented Ben with his contract.

"All has gone well, and you've successfully supplied two souls in full payment of your contract. With the, as you put it, "ransom" paid, I am honor bound to return your contract."

Smiling, Ben took the contract from Lucifer's hand and tore it in half. As the page halves separated, there was a crash from the kitchen. Lucifer vanished and Ben wheeled himself to the kitchen to find Lily lying dead on the floor.

The coroner's report stated an undiagnosed heart condition as the cause of the young girl's untimely death, but Ben knew otherwise and lived with his guilt.

Pete never did return to Westmoreland and Ben wheeled his way through life alone, never letting anyone close. He used Lily's insurance money to get him through college and into a semi-successful graphic design career, but no amount of success would erase the bitterness and guilt that dwelt in and darkened his heart. Every week he visited Sam's grave, knowing he was to blame for all that happened to her. He would cry by the grave in his wheelchair knowing all that had been lost.

The last he had seen of Lucifer was the day Lil died, but the Devil stayed on Ben's mind as grew older and more and more hateful to all around him. Everyone knew him to be the spiteful, paralyzed, hate-filled hermit who lived in a broken-down house.

The years slowly passed and as Ben approached his 56th birthday, a clot from a vein in his atrophied right leg broke free and lodged itself in his lungs. Panicked and clutching his chest, he sat in his wheelchair, wide-eyed, confused, afraid, and alone, gasping for air, until all became black.

Opening his eyes, he found himself in a familiar library. "What? What am I doing here?" he shouted as he jumped out of the leather chair and onto his feet.

"Hi, Ben, nice to see you again," said Lucifer as he stoked the fireplace.

"But my contract! I tore up my contract, our deal was nullified."

"Of course you did, and it was," said Lucifer calmly. "But you corrupted and sold out two innocent souls to do so. You see Ben, I collect souls in only one way, I get them sent to me because of their misdeeds. The opposition especially dislikes it when you corrupt innocence. You are here for that, not because of the contract. To be completely honest and in full transparency I can't buy your soul. It's not yours to barter with but you can give it to me. The contract never was binding." He added with a laugh.

"You liar! You had this planned out all along!"

"Now Ben, I never did lie to you; I just never told you the whole truth, and well, I guess I did lie to you after all. So, sue me. I do have quite a few lawyers down here. Look, I stumbled on this little pyramid idea a few years ago watching business schemes on Earth. I must say that the number of souls I've collected is skyrocketing. Why, Jennifer and Justin, the two souls you helped me with, have each already sent another two souls, and those four lead to eight and so on. Just from your unhappiness alone, I have gained sixty-two more souls already and the number just keeps on growing."

Ben just hung his head and began to cry.

"Hey, don't be so blue," laughed Lucifer. "Besides you getting your legs back, I have a surprise for you."

Ben looked up to see Lily step out from the shadows. She walked slowly towards Ben as he silently stared. She was clad only in a thin, silky red dress and was radiant. Her blonde hair was now full, long, and flaming red cascading over her smooth bare shoulders. Her blue eyes were dark with a smoldering glow. All the scars had vanished, and her skin glowed with a soft warmth.

She drew closer and her red lips slowly parted, "Hi lover. Long time no see."

Ben was surprised to notice two small half-inch horns protruding from her forehead. His surprise changed to horror as he saw two leathery bat-like wings unfold from her smooth back. As she smiled, two white fangs were clearly outlined against her crimson lips.

"What? No, she can't be...," cried Ben.

Lucifer laughed. "Ben, this is my daughter, Lilith. I know you called her Lily. She took a liking to you and wanted you for her own. What kind of father would I be if I told her no? So, I am now presenting you to her as a little present."

"She's a demon!"

A succubus to be exact," corrected the Devil. "She's quite the little torturer. Goodbye, Ben. You two kids have fun."

Charles Embrey Jr

Satan laughed as the succubus dragged Ben screaming from the library by his hair. She looked down at Ben and smiled, "Now we'll always be together, lover. Always and forever."

Always and Forever

Alternative Ending

    Several of my regular readers have noticed my ending, well, Ben's ending, wasn't exactly what they expected. They have grown accustomed to a less gut-wrenching conclusion to my stories. In that vein of thought, and because I always try to satisfy my readers, I present this alternative ending as a bonus.

Charles Embrey Jr.

Ben was enveloped in darkness, but the pain subsided. The world around him was as comforting and secure as a warm blanket except for a steady, incessant beeping. Time crept by slowly, days, weeks, or months, Ben couldn't tell. Finally, the beeping grew louder until Ben could stand it no more and his eyes burst open to see the white ceiling of a hospital room.

He reached up to find a thick tube coming from his mouth and multiple tubes attached to each arm. Rolling his head to the right, towards the source of the beeping, he saw a heart monitor showing eighty beats per minute and a blood pressure of 140 over 70. He was alive.

Over the next day or so Ben found out that although he was alive, he had suffered greatly in the accident. He had broken his back when he slammed into the steering wheel and was now paralyzed from the abdomen down, and his arms were now considerably weaker. However, on the third day after waking up, his greatest horror was realized. His parents had just left for the day, and Ben was drifting off to sleep when he was jolted back to consciousness by her voice. "Hi, lover! I thought I lost you."

He snapped his head to the doorway to see Lily limping into the room on crutches. It was Lily, but his angel also suffered from the accident. Aside from her broken leg, Ben was horrified to see her face. Multiple red scars on her forehead bore silent witness to her impact with the windshield, and large thick patches of pink skin covered the right side of her face and neck. It distorted the side of her mouth and made her right eye constantly partially closed. Most of her golden hair was gone with only patches showing any promise of returning.

Always and Forever

She sat next to him and carefully took his hand into hers. The once soft delicate skin of her hands was now rough and unyielding. "I was thrown free of the crash when we hit the bridge, but as I was pulling you free from the steering wheel the car caught fire. I guess I got a little singed, but we made it."

"A little singed?" thought Ben. To him, it looked as if she had stopped a grenade blast with her face.

"Don't worry, Ben. Your paralysis makes no difference to me. I love you and I'll look after you forever. I told your parents that we're getting married after you leave the hospital and I'll nurse you back to health."

"Please, Lil. I need to sleep. Let's talk about this tomorrow."

"Alright, lover. I'll see you tomorrow. I love you," she whispered as she brought her scarred lip to his cheek.

That night, as Ben lay quietly, his nose detected a faint smell of sulfur. Turning toward the window he spotted Lucifer sitting in the visitor's chair.

"A young, pretty, student nurse named Jennifer will be on duty taking care of you tonight. Talk her into sneaking a six-pack of beer into the hospital to share with you. You do that and I'll take care of the rest."

"I don't know if I can."

"Because you don't know how or don't want to?"

"Both really," said Ben, feeling very guilty about being responsible for corrupting someone innocent.

"Fine, you little lying prick. Spend the rest of your life with Scarface and come back to Hell when you die."

"But I'm the reason she looks like that. I hurt her."

"Sure, you did... but remember she was going to end up killing you. It was self-defense. She deserved it."

Ben thought hard. "I guess you're right, but to corrupt someone..."

"Look, did Greg hold a gun to your head and demand the tests? No, he did not! He simply put an opportunity in front of you. It was your choice to do as he asked. And your choice to sign my contract for that matter. It was always your choice. All you ever had to do was say no."

"Okay, fine, but how do I do it?"

"Now we're talking, boy. Once you get Jennifer's attention and trust, simply lay on the peer pressure."

"Peer pressure?"

"Sure, you know... It's okay, everybody does it. Don't worry, nobody's getting hurt. It's only wrong if we get caught and we'll be careful. Peer pressure has always been my greatest tool. Who do you think invented it?" said Satan with a hearty laugh.

Ben nodded and smiled weakly.

"Besides," continued Lucifer. "If you're lucky enough to pull this off, I already have a second person in mind. There's a good chance you can have your contract back by the end of the month."

Lucifer vanished, and within the hour Jenn showed up as promised.

"Knock knock," came a tender voice from the hospital door.

A second later, a fresh, pretty, smiling face, framed with soft brown, wavy, shoulder-length locks peeked through the door.

Ben's stomach hurt as he called out, "Come in."

Always and Forever

The young girl walked timidly into the room. "Hi, I'm Jennifer. I hope you don't mind, but I'm a student nurse, and I'll be taking care of you tonight."

Ben forced a smile while the pain in his stomach increased. "Hi, I'm Ben."

"I hope so," she giggled. "If not, one of us is in the wrong room."

"Yeah, sorry," he blushed. "I guess I wasn't thinking."

The young girl giggled again. "How are you feeling tonight?"

"As long as I hit this little button, I feel great," said Ben while holding up the red button on his narcotic pain pump. "But then, only half of me can feel anymore."

Jennifer's smile vanished, but she recovered just as quickly. "Ben, don't talk like that. I read in your chart that you have surgery scheduled for tomorrow to relieve pressure on your spinal cord. There is a good chance that you will get your legs back."

"I wouldn't call a 5 percent chance a 'good chance.'"

"Now stop talking like that!" she scolded, even surprising herself. "You have to believe in yourself. The surgeon can only do so much. You must do the rest."

The young man forced a weak smile. Sam would have gotten onto him just like that.

"I need to make my rounds, but after 9, I will only have you and the elderly lady in the next room to watch over. She sleeps all night. If you don't mind, I'll come back, and we can talk some more about the poor attitude."

Ben's smile grew, even as a tear fell from the corner of his right eye.

"I'm sorry. I shouldn't be so bossy."

"No," replied Ben wiping away the smile. "It's just that you remind me of an old friend."

She smiled. "He must be bossy too."

"Bossy, yes, but a girl. She died a few months ago."

She gasped and put her hand to her mouth attempting to hide her fears.

"Not the girl from the park?"

Ben nodded and another tear fell.

The young nursing student's astonishment and fear turned into resolve. "I'll be back at 9. Ben Strong, we are going to fix that attitude and have you ready for that surgery!"

"Thanks, Jennifer."

She giggled again. "Call me Jenn. All my friends do."

"Alright Jenn," said Ben, surprised to see he was now a friend.

She turned and flashed a smile as she whisked out the door.

As promised, she returned just after 9 and moved a chair next to the bed. The two sat and talked for a few hours. Ben felt totally at ease with the student nurse and soon realized that he felt better inside than he had in quite a while.

"Oh! It's 11:30," announced Jenn. She reached into her smock pocket and produced a Snickers bar. "Here," she said as she handed it to Ben. "Remember, NPO, nothing to eat or drink after midnight. You now have a half hour to eat this."

Ben grinned. "You must have heard my stomach growling."

Jenn giggled. Why Mr. Strong, you appear to be feeling better! Tomorrow is going to be a big day. I'll leave you to finish the candy bar and get some sleep."

Always and Forever

"You have to leave?"

Jenn rolled her eyes a little and smiled. "I should, but if you want me to stay a little longer, I guess it will be okay."

"Please do. I haven't felt this relaxed in months."

Jenn sat back down, her dark brown eyes catching Ben's attention. "So, how are you feeling about that 5 percent chance now?"

"It's going to work. I know it will."

The two continued talking and were shocked when the floor nurse entered the room. "Mr. Strong, the anesthesiologist will be here in a few minutes to review his preop paperwork. Jennifer, it's 3 o'clock and your shift is over."

"Mrs. Winston! I'm sorry. I lost track of time."

The nurse softly smiled. "That's quite alright, dear. I can easily see that Mr. Strong is in much better spirits. Nursing is not just about medicine and charts."

Jennifer jumped up and squeezed Ben's hand. "You'll do great. I'm working again the day after tomorrow. See you then."

Ben sighed as Jenn scurried out the door.

Nurse Winston looked over Ben's monitors. "She's right, you know," she said without looking away from the screen.

"What do you mean?"

"You'll do great. Relax, Dr Kuntz will be here soon, and I think your parents and girlfriend just got here."

'Girlfriend.' The stomachache came back with the word.

Later that afternoon, Ben woke completely disoriented. His back hurt but he still couldn't feel his legs. Tears fell as Ben's parents and Lily entered the room. Lil rushed to his side and took his hand.

"It didn't work!" cried Ben, as he looked helplessly at his parents.

Ben's father placed a reassuring hand on his son's shoulder. "Dr Kuntz felt that all went as well as it could. With the damage done and swelling from the surgery, it could be a while before we know if it was a success or not."

"How long is a while?" asked Ben hesitantly.

Mr. Strong shrugged his shoulders. It could be tomorrow or a year from now. These nerve things can be very unpredictable."

"Don't be sad, lover," said Lily with her rasping voice. "Just remember, no matter what, we have each other, always and forever."

Ben faked a smile. "I need to get some sleep now."

Mrs. Strong grabbed her son's hand. "We will take Lily home, son. Get some rest and we will be back tomorrow."

"Thanks, mom"

Lily leaned over the bed and kissed Ben with her leathery, scarred lips. "I love you," she whispered. "Don't worry, I will look after your parents. As long as you're mine, your parents will be safe."

Ben's blood ran cold as Lily drew away. "I love you too, Lil. Always and forever," he said with feigned conviction.

The next day, Ben slept most of the time Lily and his parents visited. If he wasn't truly asleep, he would fake it, to keep from talking to Lily. All he could think about that day was tomorrow's visit with Jenn. He couldn't explain it, but she brought a sense of calm to his heart, and he longed to feel that peace again. She was practically a stranger, but somehow, he felt a connection.

The next night, Jennifer entered the room, but the sense of joy Ben felt quickly evaporated and was replaced with dread. All he could feel was the selfish need to protect his parents and to get rid of Lily. He knew he would have to ask Jenn about the beer and hoped that she wouldn't be cursed as he was.

The girl could sense that something was bothering her patient but rationalized that it was still the pain and discomfort from the surgery and his worry about the delayed results.

About an hour into their conversation, Ben looked at Jennifer, his eyes wet with tears. "Can you do me a really big favor?" he asked as the cramping and emptiness replaced any joy he had left inside.

"What favor?" she asked innocently.

"This pain is relentless, and I really need to relax for at least a moment. Can you sneak a 6-pack of beer in here? It would save my life."

The young girl bit her lower lip and was about to speak when Ben burst into tears. All the emotions of the last few months came flowing out. Guilt and remorse over Sam and Pete had been eating his insides out and were now escaping.

Jennifer leaned over the bed and held Ben tightly as his body shook. Finally, his breathing slowed, and he managed to gather his racing thoughts and speak.

"I am so sorry, Jenn. Please, please, please! Don't bring me anything. Don't break any rules for me. I can't do it! I will burn in

Hell, but I can't hurt you. I won't hurt you!" Looking up at the ceiling, determination filled his youthful face. "Hear that you Bastard!? I won't hurt her!"

With all her strength, Jennifer remained calm and stroked his hair. "It's alright. I've got you. It's okay. Just relax and catch your breath. You're having a reaction to the pain meds. I'll get the nurse."

"No Jenn. It's not the meds. It's real. I mean it. You have to leave and never come to see me again. It's not safe and I can't see you hurt."

"Benjamin Strong! I'm a big girl and I won't go anywhere without an explanation. That was a powerful rush of feelings. Talk to me. Please."

"You'll think I'm crazy."

"If this burden is hurting you so badly, crazy or not, just get it out."

Ben dried his eyes and began to unburden his soul. He left nothing out and felt a peace returning with every word. Reaching the end of his confession, Ben became afraid. How could he have shared all that with a stranger?

Jennifer sat quietly for a moment absorbing all she had heard. Whether Ben was crazy or not was irrelevant. He believed it.

"I'm not going anywhere, Ben. I don't know if everything you said is true or not, but I do know that you honestly believe that you will burn in Hell for all eternity for saving me. That is the purest and most powerful love anyone could have for another. I am here and I'm not leaving. Now, what can we do to fix this?"

For the first time since meeting Lucifer, hope returned and swelled Ben's heart. "I have to get Lily out of my life, and she has to pay for what she did to Sam."

Always and Forever

"Apparently she didn't leave any evidence behind," observed Jennifer.

"Yeah, but when we are alone, she doesn't hide it. I think she is proud of what she did and uses it to keep me in line."

"Then we record it," announced Jennifer.

"Tomorrow. Let's do it tomorrow, but we must do it right. We need that detective that arrested Pete."

"I would leave out the devil part of your story, but I agree," said Jenn. "I'll go out to the desk and call. Do you remember the detective's name?"

"Crap! Wait…it's… Farmer. Detective Farmer! That's it."

The detective sounded skeptical on the phone, but the case had grown cold and he was hoping for any break. He entered the hospital room an hour later looking a little sleepy.

Ben explained everything while Jennifer held his hand for support. If the detective was drowsy when he arrived, he was wide awake now.

Late-night phone calls rocked several technical agents from their beds and plans were quickly made for a microphone near Ben. An observation and recording room was set up in a vacant patient's room just down the hall.

"Look detective, when she confesses, you must protect my parents. You can't let her leave here."

"Don't worry. If we get a confession, she will not set foot outside this hospital without handcuffs," promised Detective Farmer.

The next day, Lily and the Strongs arrived at the hospital happy to see Ben more awake and alert.

After about an hour, Ben asked his parents if he could have a little time alone to talk with Lily. Mr. Strong winked at his wife and the two left to grab some lunch.

Lily was elated to hear Ben ask for time alone with her. Grabbing his hand, she leaned over and kissed his cheek. "Let's get married after you leave the hospital."

Ben smiled, "I'd like that, but I was completely spaced out the other day when you left the hospital. Did you say something about watching over my parents?"

Lily's eyes narrowed and then she grinned broadly. "We are getting married. You're all mine now. They are safe."

"But I'm worried. What if someone tries to come between us?"

The grin vanished and Lily's face became stone. No one will come between us. No one ever! I can see to that. Remember?"

"Oh, you mean Sam?"

"Sam! Yeah. She wanted to take you away! That little bitch tried to convince me that she would leave you alone. She cried and said that I was all yours. I looked right into her lying eyes as I caved her head in with that mower blade. Damn right, you're mine and I'll kill anyone that tries to take you from me."

"It's all okay now, sweetheart. I'm yours."

"I buried that bitch's heart under Pete's shed. I hoped he would fry for it but, well, he left town so he's safe now."

"I'm yours. You don't have to worry."

"You're not mad?"

"Why? You did it to protect us. I couldn't be mad at you. Why don't you run and find out about a marriage license? We can get married here in the hospital."

Always and Forever

Lily jumped up with excitement and kissed Ben. "You are the greatest! I can't wait. I'll be back soon."

Lily ran out of the room and into Detective Farmer and ten uniformed officers. The scuffle and screams could be heard through much of the hospital wing.

Detective Farmer entered Ben's room as the screams echoed down the hall, steadily getting further down the hall. His shirt was torn and deep scratches across his face were bleeding onto his collar.

"Thank you, Ben," said the detective as he gasped for air. "She is in chains, but damn, she's strong. You did the right thing."

"Finally," said Ben. His soul still belonged to Satan but at least Lily was out of his life and nobody else would be hurt.

A few hours later, Jennifer came rushing into the room. "It's all over the news! She was laughing at the news camera as they were taking her into the jail. She kept screaming, "Ben is mine. Always and forever. You'll all see, Ben is mine and there is nothing he can do about it!"

Ben's blood ran cold, but the woman was locked up. He was finally free. Smiling at Jennifer he calmly said, "Thank you."

Early the next morning, Ben woke to the sound of the hospital alarm and footsteps running down the hall. Hospital security burst into the room. One man secured the windows and drew all the blinds closed. Another cleared the restroom as two men placed themselves on either side of Ben's bed.

"What is going on?" exclaimed Ben as he felt his blood pressure rise with the rush of adrenalin.

"I'm not sure", replied the older guard next to the bed. "All I know is that the police called and ordered a lockdown. We are to protect you at all costs."

When the hospital alarm quieted, Ben could hear the police sirens growing louder from the distance.

Within 5 minutes, Detective Farmer burst into the hospital room. "Thank God you're safe," he said trying to catch his breath. "Has Lily contacted you?"

"Contacted me? You have her in jail!"

Farmer grimaced, "Had her in jail. This morning the cell was locked but empty. On surveillance cameras, she was there, and, well, then she wasn't."

Ben started looking about in panic. "My parents! You must protect them."

"Already done. We have mobilized all officers on the force. They are going door to door. We will find her. I will leave an armed officer here outside your door, but I have to go back out and help the search."

Ben settled nervously back on his pillow. He didn't care what happened to him anymore as long as his family was safe.

Throughout the morning and into the afternoon Ben could hear an occasional siren racing down the street. After his lunch tray was picked up, he settled back and dozed off in the warm room. His fitful dream was interrupted by a familiar voice that chilled him to his core.

"Hey, Lover! Did you miss me?"

Ben's eyes opened wide and frantically scanned the room. He was alone and he could see the police officer sitting quietly outside his room. Realizing it was just a bad dream he laid back and let out a sigh. Suddenly, a faint odor of sulfur stung his nose and a second familiar voice called out, only this time Ben was fully awake.

Always and Forever

"Ben...Ben...Ben. I just don't know what I will do with you," chuckled Lucifer as he stepped from the shadow.

"Get away from me!" shouted Ben. "Help!"

Satan laughed loudly and in a mocking tone that frightened Ben. "The guard can't hear you. Not while I want us to have some 'alone' time. I can't believe you wussed out on saving yourself. You could have been home free but look at you now."

"I don't care!" shouted Ben. I made my choice. I made it and I'll live with it."

"Wow, little Ben grew a pair. Yell at me all you want. I still own you and, well, I have someone here that wants to say 'hi'".

A smaller form slipped from the shadows beside Lucifer. She was slender and dressed in a sheer red gown. Dark red hair with lighter red highlights flowed from her crown and draped across and down her shoulders almost giving the appearance of flame. Her alabaster skin was flawless accentuating her dark, almost black, eyes and crimson-red lips. It was Lily!

Her red lips teased a smile, "Hi, Lover. Did you miss me?" Seeing Ben's horrified expression, her smile grew, and two bright-white fangs stood in sharp contrast against her lower lip. Ben's horror escaped his lips as two leathery, bat-like wings unfolded from her back.

"You're a demon!"

"I am not!" scolded Lily, notably offended.

"Stay calm, dear," scolded Satan. "She is a succubus, Ben. And most importantly, my daughter. You knew her as Lily, but her true name is Lilith. Be proud of yourself Ben. Of all the mortals she took a liking to you."

Lilith smiled again, "You're mine, Ben. Daddy has your contract and when you die, and you will, we will be together, always and forever, like you promised."

"Forever, Ben," added Satan. "And I can guarantee that my Lilith has no interest in snuggling. She is quite the little torturer. I'm so proud."

"See you soon, Lover. We are going to have so much fun. Well, I guess, I'll be the one having fun. You…well, not so much."

Lilith and Lucifer vanished, and Ben found it hard to breathe as panic gripped his chest tighter than a vice. Laying there in bed, he cried knowing that his fate was now sealed.

Jennifer found him despondent when her shift started. Try as she might, she couldn't get through the wall of despair he had surrounded himself with. After about a week of patiently encouraging him, he started to crack a smile, but it broke into a full grin the next night when he felt his toes tingling.

As he struggled to regain his ability to walk, he resigned himself to his fate and decided to find his happiness in this life. During the months of rehab, he and Jenn grew closer and closer. One afternoon, during his exercises, Ben's legs shook, and he fell to his knees at Jennifer's feet.

The startled girl quickly reached down to help, but Ben looked up grinning and holding a diamond ring!

Ben worked harder and a few months later stood on his own at the altar as Jennifer was walked down the aisle by her father.

Ben had finally found happiness but occasionally, in the quiet of night, he would see Sam in the back of his mind and the guilt would overtake him, eating at his insides and his spirit would sink into the

Always and Forever

dark abyss. Knowledge of Satan's contract hanging over his head, often caused panic attacks and bags under his eyes stood as witness to sleepless nights.

Becoming a father added to his joy and panic attacks became less frequent. Jennifer was happy to see her husband finally able to sleep through the night from time to time.

Life was now filled with work, school projects, baseball games and walks with his wife.

Tragedy struck when Jenn was late coming home from the grocery store one night. Waiting for her on the front porch, Ben, now 51 years old, felt the emptiness again enter his stomach when the police car pulled up at his house.

A traffic accident had robbed him of his love. Hope faded and night terrors returned. Clinging to his grown children kept him reasonably sane but the birth of his first grandchild made him cry with joy. Unfortunately, even all of this could never truly replace the love of the woman who saved his life.

Years of stress and guilt had taken their toll, and one warm spring morning, Ben felt tightness in his chest growing stronger and stronger, pushing up into his neck and jaw. Visions of waiting hellfire filled his terrified mind and he was barely able to dial 9-1-1 before darkness overtook him.

Ben opened his eyes to find himself in a green, lush countryside. A cool breeze complimented the warm sun shining overhead in a calm blue sky. All his pain had vanished, and his legs felt stronger than ever.

A feeling of peace washed over him as he spied an older man tending a garden just ahead. The scent of honeysuckle filled his nostrils during the short walk to the garden's gate.

At the gate, Ben could see the lush tomato plants and cucumber vines laden with produce as well as many other plants and flowers. The gardener had well-groomed hair and a short beard of the purest white.

"Good morning, sir," said Ben as he looked over the closed gate.

The gentleman stood and opened the gate. His violet eyes caught Ben's attention. An overwhelming feeling of love swept over him. "Hello, Ben. Welcome!" he exclaimed before giving him a warm hug.

"You know me?" said Ben surprised. "Where am I?"

The man smiled warmly, "What is the last thing you remember, son?"

Ben thought hard for a moment and remembered the chest pain. "Am I dreaming?"

"Not quite."

"Then I'm dead?"

The man smiled and touched his nose before turning back to the tomatoes.

"I can't be dead," said Ben in a panic. "I'm supposed to be in Hell."

"Now who told you that?" the man replied with a soft chuckle.

"Satan did! He has my contract. I sold my soul."

"Ben," replied the man with a twinkle in his violet eyes and a warm smile. "Don't you know he lies? You would have thought the title 'Father of all Lies' would give that away. Lies all the time, that snake," chuckled Heavenly Father. "Ben, there is no contract, never was. He never did buy your soul. Truth is, it's not yours to sell. My eldest Son purchased it long before you were born. That's why you are here."

Always and Forever

"This is Heaven?"

"Well, it's not Iowa," he said with a laugh.

"Then you're…"

"Yes, Ben. I'm God but I really prefer being called Heavenly Father."

"But how? I did those bad things. I killed Sam."

"True, but you did lots of good things too, and you didn't kill Sam. Lilith did."

"Thank you but I didn't do anything all that special. I do have a question though. All those times Satan was visiting me and trying to convince me to do bad things, why didn't you visit me too?

Heavenly Father smiled warmly, "Who do you think made your stomach hurt so badly? I don't work the way Satan does. I want it to be you that decides what path you follow. When you rejected Satan and sacrificed yourself to save Jennifer, well, that opened this gate to you. Oh, speaking of Sam and Jennifer, well, I think the reunion is long overdue.

Ben looked up to see the two women smiling and laughing as they ran across the field to greet him.

Tears of joy flowed down his cheeks as he looked back at his Heavenly Father. "Thank you," he whispered. "Thank you!"

Made in the USA
Middletown, DE
01 July 2024